# GHOSTS AND LEGENDS
# OF THE LAKE DISTRICT

# Ghosts and Legends of the Lake District

By J.A. Brooks

*The Genii that haunt the romantic valleys, the hills, woods and rivers of Cumberland and Westmorland, are so mischievous and malevolent in their disposition, so terrific in their aspect, and hostile to the human race, that a person would be thought very regardless of his safety, were he to entrust himself at any late hour of the night in the neighbourhood of their haunts.*

(Robert Anderson, *The Burns of Cumberland, c.*1770–1833.)

Jarrold Colour Publications, Norwich

*I am grateful to the following librarians for the assistance they gave me in researching the text and illustrations for this book:*

Dr S.T.Chapman, The Armitt Library, Ambleside;
Mr Stephen White, The Cumbrian Collection, Carlisle;
Mr Trevor Jones, Local History Librarian, Workington.

Picture Credits

Cover illustration: The Langdale Pikes, chromolithograph by J.B.Pyne

ISBN 0-7117-0340-x
© 1988 Jarrold Colour Publications
Printed and published in Great Britain by Jarrold and Sons Ltd, Norwich. 1/88

# Contents

## Bibliography

| | |
|---|---|
| W.G. Collingwood | The Lake Counties, 1932 |
| A.H. Griffin | In Mountain Lakeland, 1963 |
| William Rollinson | Life and Tradition in the Lake District, 1974 |
| John Parker | Cumbria, 1977 |
| A.H. Griffin | The Roof of England, 1968 |
| Hunter Davies | A Walk around the Lakes, 1979 |
| W.T. Palmer | In Lakeland Dells and Fells, 1903 |
| A. Wainwright | A Pictorial Guide to the Lakeland Fells, 1-7, 1955-66 |
| A. Wainwright | Fellwalking with Wainwright, 1984 |
| Elliott O'Donnell | Haunted Britain, 1948 |
| Brian Branston | The Lost Gods of England, 1957 |
| Thomas Carrick | The Borderland in the Olden Times, 1903 |
| Jeremiah Sullivan | Cumberland and Westmorland Ancient & Modern, 1857 |
| Jessica Lofthouse | North Country Folklore, 1976 |
| Norman Nicholson | The Lakes, 1955 |
| Wilson Armistead | Tales and Legends of the English Lakes, 1891 |
| Thomas Gibson | Legends of North Westmorland, 1887 |
| William Henderson | Notes on the Folklore of the Northern Counties of England, 1866 |
| Jessica Lofthouse | The Curious Traveller through Lakeland, 1954 |
| F.J. Carruthers | Lore of the Lake District, 1975 |
| Marjorie Rowling | The Folklore of the Lake District, 1976 |
| William Hutchinson | History of Cumberland, 1794-7 |
| Gerald Findler | Lakeland Ghosts, 1969 |
| Augustus Hare | The Story of My Life, 1896 |

Chapter One

# The Hills are Haunted . . .

In these pages I have cast my net wide: here the Lake District embraces an area from Arnside in the south to the Scottish Border in the north. In breadth it extends from the coast of the Solway Firth to the slopes of the Pennines in the east. I have covered this large area because there are hosts of interesting hauntings to be found on the periphery, many of them complementing the stories of the ghosts of Lakeland proper.

I have quoted frequently from my sources, because the prose written in times past was generally much more evocative for tales involving the Unknown, and conveys atmosphere and a genuine sense of involvement. Most of these stories come to us having been told very many times before, so it is as well to reach as far back as possible.

Ghost stories come into being in a variety of ways. At the heart of many, there must be a kernel of truth, some incident that cannot be explained away by natural agencies. Many of us have had such experiences, the most common being the sense of déjà-vu, the feeling that 'all this has happened to me before'. Then there are events which defy rational explanation – a scent in a place known to be absolutely isolated and unvisited, or that grim feeling of being under observation when working alone in an old and deserted building. You have to turn around sometime yet you dread doing so – the nameless horror syndrome.

Thus, having accepted that things can happen to us that we are unable to explain even to ourselves, we can listen to the stories of other people with a fair degree of sympathy. The trouble is that such stories, many of them first told centuries ago when the wonder of the experience was still fresh, have suffered embroidery over the years so that the magical *inexplicable* part of the story is camouflaged by romance and allegory. Most legends probably began with a liberal helping of the supernatural: it was the only way to make the story memorable.

Then there are the ghost stories fabricated deliberately for some

'Smugglers...also invented ghosts.'

purpose or another. Some ghosts were even invented for political purposes – Royalist ghosts would dash around market-places tripping people up and upsetting stalls, while the tale told against the Philipsons about the Calgarth Skulls may well have been made up by their Cromwellian opponents.

Smugglers and moonshiners (the latter particularly in the Lakes) also invented ghosts so that people would be frightened of investigating lonely places where their operations might be based. On the remote shore at Silverdale there were supposed to be a variety of dobbies that would see off the over-curious. Near Lindeth there was the Scout Dobbie, a headless woman who guarded a cave called Jack Scout, and there are stories of similar macabre figures patrolling cliffs and beaches all around the English coastline.

Dobbies are just one of the colloquial forms of ghost native to Cumbria. They were a comparatively friendly type of ghost (more of a household fairy or hobgoblin) compared with the more fearsome boggle or boggart. If a farm was fortunate enough to harbour a dobbie then it was easy enough to keep its services. All that was required was to set out a bowl of milk and an oat cake each evening, or a helping of curds and cream. In return for this humble offering the dobbie would help the servants with their work and make sure that the household operated smoothly. However if the dobbie fell out with the farmer through his neglect in failing to put out the token of food, then things would go badly with the work of the farm. The cheese might turn mouldy or refuse to set, the butter could go sour in the churn, and pots burn on the stove.

Although it seems that it was comparatively easy to domesticate a dobbie, apparently there was no way to tame a boggle.

> There is no nook of the country inaccessible to boggles, no mind so incredulous that it may not at some moment, or in some way, be converted from its scepticism. We have stories of persons who, on being warned of the danger of passing certain haunted places, snapped their fingers at the spirit, but – after that night were never known to speak disrespectfully of ghosts. Generally, indeed, the enlightened hold the apparition of spirits to be an impossibility. But as this in a great measure depends on the nature and extent of their philosophy, any change, or even one step farther, may carry them over this barrier, into a region where such things are quite possible.

These are the words of Jeremiah Sullivan, writing in 1857. His book, *Cumberland and Westmorland Ancient and Modern*, is a valuable source for old stories and customs. He continues:

> As the word boggle includes all the varieties of the apparition kind that preceded it, so nothing is more uncertain than the manner in which the spirit manifests itself. Any shape, human, or animal, or composite, any unaccountable noise, may be a *boggle*. . . .
> Some incredulous individuals there are who may consider unsatisfactory the evidence on the boggle cases narrated; all such are requested to read the story of the Henhow boggle, the truth of which they may ascertain by a little inquiry. It happened about twenty-three years ago. The man to whom the boggle appeared was living in Martindale, at a cottage called Henhow. His wife had heard some unaccountable noise in or around the house and had informed her husband, but no further notice was taken. One morning he had to go to his work at an early hour, and having several miles to walk, he started soon after midnight. He had not got above two hundred yards from the house, when the dog by which he was accompanied, gave signs of alarm. He looked round – at the other side of the wall that bounded the road, appeared a woman, keeping pace with him, and carrying a child in her

Mill Beck and Buttermere Chapel

arms. There was no means of escape; he spoke to the figure, and asked her 'what was troubling her?' Then she told him her story. She had once lived at Henhow, and had been seduced. Her seducer, to cloak his guilt and her frailty, met her by appointment at a certain market-town, and gave her a medicine, the purpose of which is obvious. It proved too potent, and killed both mother and child. Her doom was to wander thus for a hundred years, forty of which were already expired. On his return home at night, the man told what he had seen and heard; and when the extraordinary story spread through the dale, the 'old wives' were able to recall some almost forgotten incidents precisely identical with those related by the boggle. The seducer was known to be a clergyman. The occurrence is believed to have made a lasting impression on the old man, who still lives, and was until very lately a shepherd on the fells. There can be no moral doubt that he both saw, and spoke with, the boggle; but what share his imagination had therein, or how it had been excited, are mysteries, and so they are likely to remain.

Jessica Lofthouse, in *North Country Folklore*, makes the important distinction between the boggles of Cumbria and the boggarts of

Lancashire, the latter seeming to be closely related to the dobbie:

> *(The boggart)* ... could be sly, full of mischievous pranks, his nuisance value high. But he rarely did serious harm and was so often helpful in the 'good brownie' family tradition that he was usually tolerated.
>
> When visible, a boggart was seen to be half man – the half spirit was his unseen self – no more than knee high, his face wizened, his neck scrawny like an old man's, his arms thin, his legs looking incapable of supporting his corpulent body. In bad mood his face was contorted as in a rage: when indulging in pranks he grinned with impish glee; in good mood his mien was benevolent.

Miss Lofthouse goes on to point out that the boggart hardly exists north of the old Lancashire border (thus one might just encounter a rare specimen in southern Lakeland). In Cumbria the less friendly boggle has taken over, with the boggart being more commonly known as the dobbie. The word 'boggle' derives from the Norse word *bwg*, frighten, which reached other parts of the country far away from Cumbria. As a child with parents from the fens of East Anglia I can remember being told that I had the Bogey-Man on my back if I was being more difficult than usual. But to return to *North Country Folklore*:

> ... With boggarts there was always a chance they were in a good mood; one experienced just a slight tingling of fear. With boggles it was different, spine-chilling to encounter one. A boggle was a vague, often faceless creature, a light, a ball of fire, a ghostly shape, a phantom hound or bull or calf, or red hen or black cock. They often had to keep watch over hidden treasure. They could uncover the graves of the dead. ... But they harmed none of the pure in heart, or honest and upright folk. Evil they could smell out a mile away, track down relentlessly the guilty, 'all murderers, mansworn, and those who preyed upon widows and orphans...'

Perhaps the last word on boggles is best left with Jeremiah Sullivan:

> Though it would be unsafe to declare the entire extinction of boggles, it is certain they have very sensibly declined. The boggles of the present day are scarcely more than the ghosts of boggles. ...

It will be seen from the pages that follow that the Lake District cannot boast of too many ghost stories of the present day. It is difficult to account for this: the romantic landscape has been the scene of countless accidents and sudden death is usually held responsible for restless spirits. There have been fatal mishaps to aeroplanes as well as parties of climbers, yet ghostly reminders of these seem remarkably thin on the ground. Perhaps the stories are told yet not recorded, which would be a pity. There are even very few instances of the famous Brocken Spectre having being seen: in Scotland as in most mountainous regions of Europe this strange trick of the light is regularly encountered.

Griffin says that he has seen it twice, on one occasion on Lingmell and once on the Buttermere fells. As one approaches a skyline, your own figure may appear, magnified many times and in silhouette against the clouds behind the ridge of a neighbouring summit. It may take a moment or two to realise that this is just a freakish projection of oneself. No wonder it was a terrifying experience for early climbers!

The following account of the phenomenon dates from 1854, though the episode itself took place more than thirty years earlier. The writer and two friends set out to climb Skiddaw from Cockermouth early in the morning of 4 October 1820.

Buttermere from Honister Crag

We walked to Bassenthwaite, about seven miles. We ascended Skiddaw on that side, which is more steep than the ascent from Keswick, being about three miles to the summit.

The morning was fine until we had completed about one-third of our way up, when we were suddenly surprised by rain and we could no longer see the fine prospect around us. We had no guide, and had got upon some swampy ground, which made me consider it unsafe to go on, and I proposed to return.

However his companions persuaded the writer to continue the climb, and they decided to visit an old friend at Red House (near Millbeck, to the south of the mountain). To do this they came down by Ullock Pike

... on the right of which, as you descend, is a terrific chasm, on whose border we had to walk on a line with each other: and I think at the time we were about six yards apart. On the left we had a declivity of greensward; we were obliged to step carefully for our own safety; and could not, therefore, look around us.

Suddenly we perceived this great cavity to be fearfully gloomy, as if filled with a dense fog, or by something we did not comprehend, and the dark gigantic figure of a man, as standing on a cloud, right before us in the centre of a luminous ring of about twelve feet diameter, of the most vivid prismatic colours of the rainbow, and at the apparent distance of about ten yards, the circle extending about two feet above the head and the like beneath the feet. For the moment we were awe-stricken. My friend exclaimed, 'Tremendous! Just like Jesus Christ!'

There was now a silent pause, but in a minute we looked calmly on the figure before us, and still considered it independent of ourselves − that is, we had nothing to do with its formation.

It was then two o'clock. The sun shone brightly on where we stood, and his rays passed us into the dark abyss at the oblique angle consequent on the time of the year and on the time of the day. One of us accidentally made some gesticulation, and saw that the figure did likewise, and then called out, 'It's my figure'. Another, holding up his hand said, 'No, it's mine' and so said the third. Thus we found that although one figure only was visible to all of us, yet that was a magnified one of himself, and that the beautiful circular iris was reflected to his own eye alone, and, had there been twenty of us, each and all would have seen but one appearance.

The whole, I think, lasted not more than five or six minutes, when the

13

Thirlwall Castle, Cumberland

vivid colours gradually faded, the opaque figure began to be transparent, and the gulf again clear as the scenery around us. My idea is that this effect might possibly be the result of a fleecy cloud, such as we had frequently seen that day, of a sufficient density to refract the sun's rays and operate as a concave mirror to give back the human forms magnified to about eight feet in height.

There has always been witchcraft and wizardry in Lakeland. Even today there are flourishing covens here, and in 1984 one of the best-known modern witches, Eleanor Bone, presided over the funeral service of her husband when he was buried in Garrigill cemetery. This was the first time that a witch had officiated at a funeral in this country.

The most famous wizard, or wise-man, of the district was Dr Lickbarrow who lived in Longsleddale in about the middle of the eighteenth century. One story told of him is that even though he practised the black arts he was a regular chapelgoer. One Sunday morning he was listening to the rambling, hour-long sermon of the local parson when a sudden storm got up. Slates blew from the roof of the chapel and branches fell from the surrounding trees.

> ... The doctor, meanwhile, looked like one who felt that there was mischief abroad, and comprehended the quarter from whence it sprung. At length he hastily quitted his place, and took the road home.... He hurried onwards into his parlour, to the window of which his book of books was chained, and there found his man busily engaged in reading. The unfortunate wight had just taken a peep through curiosity, and felt compelled, in spite of himself, to read on. The doctor flung him out of the room, and sat down to the book himself, when the wind was allayed, and things returned to their usual course.
> (Jeremiah Sullivan, 1857, *Cumberland and Westmorland Ancient and Modern.*)

Sullivan continues by relating how the powers of the doctor were called upon to find lost or stolen goods.

> ... but his fame is probably founded on his success in the art of quack doctoring. As he lay on his death-bed, two pigeons, a white one and a black one, were observed fighting on the roof of his house. He took a deep interest in the progress of the combat, and when at length informed that the black bird had killed its antagonist, he ejaculated, 'It's all over with me, then!' and soon after expired.

The most famous of Lakeland witches was Margaret Teasdale who died at the age of ninety-eight and is buried in the churchyard at Over Denton. Sir Walter Scott is said to have based the character of Tib Mumps in *Guy Mannering* on this disreputable old hag, crediting her with using the sinister Hand of Glory (made from all sorts of repugnant ingredients, including the fat of a suckling child, and the severed hand of a murderer) in her criminal activities: the Hand held a specially-made candle said to possess the power of keeping a household asleep while burglars worked undisturbed. Certainly when her cottage was opened up after her death in 1777 various macabre discoveries were made, amongst them the skeleton of a child and the bones of a hand. On her tombstone is this epitaph:

> *What I was once, some may relate,*
> *What I am now is each man's fate;*
> *What I may be, none can explain,*
> *Till he that called me, calls again.*

Lizzie Baty, who lived at Brampton and died there in 1817 at the age of eighty-eight, was described as 'a canny auld body' who usually wore a red cloak and hood, trimmed with fur. She was a helpful witch in the main, always willing to lend her magic to tasks such as seeking out lost articles or giving advice on family matters. However she was also capable of using her powers to discipline those that she considered needed a lesson in manners. Once she set two cheeky young girls to laugh and dance for days on end after they had been insolent to her. On the day that she was buried one of the worst storms in living memory burst over Brampton. It became so dark that lanterns had to be used by the graveside, and they kept being blown out by the furious wind. All this was accompanied by thunder and lightning, and to add to the drama a young man named Pickering slipped and fell into the grave.

Mary Baynes of Tebay was also notorious for her magical powers. She died in 1811, aged ninety, and probably her reputation owed as much to her extreme ugliness as it did to the success of the spells she cast. She had

> . . . a nose of unproportionable length, with many crooks and turnings, adorned with great pimples which like vapours of brimstone gave strong lustre to the night. Also great goggling eyes, very sharp and fiery, and her body very long and big boned.

Like many of her kind, she was able to transmogrify herself when she pleased, often using the shape of a hare to escape pursuers. The smell of brimstone kept visitors from her cottage, with the menacing cats, 'black as jet', that prowled about the place. One of these failed to escape from the dog owned by the landlord of the local inn, the Cross Keys. The landlord, remorseful, told his servant to take the dead cat back to Mary and bury it in her garden. The man must have thought this a needless task, and when asked by the old crone to read words out of one of her books as a form of committal, he picked up the animal by one leg and recited an impromptu verse of his own:

> *Ashes to ashes, dust to dust,*
> *Here's a hole, and go thou must.*

This so angered the witch that she promised that she would be even

'The smell of brimstone kept visitors from her cottage.'

with the man, and sure enough when he was ploughing shortly afterwards he struck a sudden obstacle that caused the handle of the plough to strike him between the eyes, blinding him. There was one sure way of causing a witch such distress that she would recant the spells she had cast. This was described by Thomas Gibson in 1887 in his *Legends & Historical Notes of North Westmorland*:

> We were acquainted with a schoolmaster who roasted the heart of a chicken stuck full of pins, with fastened doors, at midnight, and he vowed that the witch came to his door and pitifully entreated him to desist, and promised she would not molest him again. Her offence was that she had bewitched a calf, so that it died, and the schoolmaster, (no fool either in other matters) thoroughly believed it.

Witches were also fond of making prophesies, not all of them successful (one Cumbrian witch forecast that the world would end in 1881). However the Witch of Tebay's vision that 'carriages without horses shall run over Loups Fell' came true when the Lancaster & Carlisle Railway was built over Shap in the 1840s, within a generation of her death.

As an ironic postscript, this report appeared in the *Westmorland Gazette* in 1983:

Railway enthusiast David Johnson saw nothing unusual when he photographed an old steam train on a lonely stretch of the main line at Tebay.

But when he got home to develop the film of the Britannia-class loco he got the shock of his life.

For standing on the embankment was a mysterious cloaked figure of a woman – who hadn't been there when he took the photograph.

Mr Johnson was convinced that the mysterious train-spotter was Mary Baines, checking, perhaps, that her prophesy really had come true.

Chapter Two

# The Southern Gateway

At first sight Arnside and Silverdale is a district which would seem to lie outside the Lake District proper. However this isolated tract of country, bordered to the east by the M6 and to the north by the estuary of the River Kent, is a part of the Lake District National Park. Those who choose to spend a few hours exploring here will be reminded of the scenery of central Lakeland (though on a smaller scale) but will always be aware of its distinct character. It is, to borrow Norman Nicholson's words, cold and bony country, a place where the rock (limestone) begins to show its teeth.

In the midst of this lies Hayes Water − the largest of the four tarns of the district, famous for its char (a fish belonging to the trout family which only lives in mountain lakes and is a great delicacy of the Lakes) and for its dragon. In bygone days this would occasionally stir the waters of the tarn into a frenzy − a portent of trouble coming to the neighbourhood. Marjorie Rowling, in *The Folklore of the Lake District*, remarks on the coincidence that in medieval times the nearby village of Yealand Conyers belonged to a daughter of William de Lancaster who married Roger of Conyers, a famous slayer of dragons from County Durham. He was often called to rid villages of the 'worms' which frequented deep, dark pools, and only emerged to seize unwary children or maidens. Ms Rowling wonders whether Roger might have managed to take a baby 'worm' alive and take it to Hayes Water as a reminder of his days as a hero. Of course if he had put more than one in the tarn all those years ago the place would be alive with dragons now!

Beetham is about three miles to the north-east of Hayes Water. The village is famous for a beauty-spot called the Fairy Steps − a staircase of natural rock which only a fairy could squeeze through with ease. Norman Nicholson remembers that his grandmother used to speak of seeing fairies in this grotto, and certainly few other settings could be more appropriate. But there is also a less welcome supernatural visitor here − the Cappel, a ghostly black dog, which terrified many late

Beetham

travellers with its blazing eyes and terrible ferocity. It lived in a barn at
Cappleside Hall, helping the farmer who sheltered it there and seeing
off all visitors, locals and strangers alike. It was even heard to talk to its
master, an unworldly attribute which may have been the reason for
the vicar being called upon to exorcise the creature, which he did,
committing it eternally to the waters of the Bela River. Cappels are the
North Country equivalent of the southern Black Shucks, and are most
common in Yorkshire.

Cappleside Hall fell into ruin at the end of the seventeenth century,
and only its tower was standing when George Hilton hid there after
the rout of the Jacobites at Preston in 1715. It has been suggested that
the legend of the black dog derives from this time, created to
discourage the curious from examining the ruins too closely. The
'Cappleside Lady' was also said to haunt the ruins, but what she looked
like and the reason for her being a ghost are both unknown. Only one
wall of the tower survives today, incorporated into another building.

Until the coming of the railways, the main route to and from the
Lake District and West Cumbria was by way of the coast. In the

21

The Fairy Steps

Middle Ages heavily-laden pack-horses would be driven up and down this route, making hazardous crossings of the innumerable creeks and estuaries which indent the coastline. Apart from the dangers of being cut off by the tide flowing up the steep-sided gullies far quicker than a man could run, there were also ever-shifting quicksands to trap the unwary. Even in the nineteenth century these routes were being used by travellers going to and from Furness. The wise old drovers had a sure way of avoiding the perils of tides and quicksands: their clever dogs were able to take the sheep or cattle across the estuaries without the help of humans who would use the safer, though longer, inland paths.

The River Kent was one of the inlets that had to be crossed in this way. The fainter-hearted would travel north to pass over the bridge at Levens. The entrance to Levens Hall is a short distance before this bridge. The most ancient, fortified, part of the house dates from the fourteenth century, though the greater part of the building-work took place in Tudor times.

As befits a house with such a romantic appearance, and with 700

Crossing the estuary

years of continuous human habitation behind it, Levens is haunted by a variety of ghosts. Particularly active is a black, woolly dog which runs in front of visitors threatening to trip them at every step. Sometimes he appears to a person when they are in company, but only one person at a time ever sees him. The dog disappears by running into a bedroom and though this is searched from floor to ceiling, no trace of the dog is ever found. Some of the distinguished musicians who visit the house have encountered the canine ghost, amongst them Raymond Leppard and Miss Zuzana Rujickova.

Another ghost who has made several appearances during the present century is the Pink Lady. She wears a dress with a pink print pattern and a mob cap. Her hauntings are random and do not seem to portend any particular doom or happiness to the family.

Levens Park, described in an early guide to the Lakes as 'the sweetest spot that Fancy can imagine', has its ghosts too. The black fallow deer that graze here are not actually black but a darkish brown. Legend has it that when a white fawn is born into the herd an important change will come to the fortunes of the estate.

Levens Hall

More sinister is the Grey Lady, the ghost of a gipsy woman who died of starvation having sought charity at Levens in the early eighteenth century. She cursed its occupants saying that there would be no son to inherit until the year when the River Kent ceased to flow and a white fawn was born in the Park. The curse was successful until 1895 when Alan Desmond Bagot was born: in that year a hind gave birth to a white fawn and the river froze solid.

The Grey Lady still makes occasional appearances to members of the family, despite the ending of her curse. The guidebook mentions a seven-year-old daughter of the house meeting her in 1954. The girl described the clothes she wore in detail. This not only matched previous sightings of the ghost but also reflected the likely apparel of a gipsy beggar-woman of the period. There are also reports of the Grey Lady and the little black dog distracting drivers on the busy main road that runs by the demesne.

The gipsy woman's poor welcome at Levens must have been unusual. Most visitors were given a great measure of the famous Morocco ale that was brewed at the house, and allowed to mature for twenty-one years (the ale, not the visitors!). The Morocco was offered in one of the 'Levens Constables', enormous old glasses that are on show at the Hall today. The toast having been said ('Luck to Levens whilst t'Kent flows') the visitor had to finish the ale without taking breath. He was then asked to walk in a straight line across the bowling green; this was seldom accomplished, and if he failed he had to pay a forfeit. Should he manage the straight line, he was given another glass of Morocco and after this few managed even to walk, let alone in a straight line.

Gaythorne Hall is another Tudor house belonging to the Levens estate. It does not strictly belong to this chapter, being situated high on the moors off the road from Tebay to Appleton. Like Levens, Gaythorne dates from the Middle Ages, with its walls many feet thick to withstand the forays of the Scots. Below ground level there were cattle byres and the infamous 'dungeon of the hairy man'. This was a cramped cell lit by a high window just twelve inches square. No-one remembers for certain the identity of 'the hairy man', but it seems that some poor soul was committed to this dungeon as a child, only to emerge years later, as an adult, perhaps wild in behaviour as well as in appearance. The reason for his captivity will never be known for certain – was he a bastard who threatened the family's respectability and its fortune? Or was he a frightening half-wit, rightful heir to the estate, in the model of the so-called Monster of Glamis?

The Dungeon of the Hairy Man, Gaythorne Hall

The present occupant of Gaythorne told me an alternative version of the legend. In the sixteenth century a child was born to parents who had made a mixed marriage: one was Protestant, the other Catholic. Because they were unable to agree on the faith that the child should be brought up in, the unfortunate boy was locked away in the cramped dungeon for many years. One day, when he was seventeen years old, the hunt passed the house and its master caught a glimpse of a pale hand waving at the little window. He discovered the boy in his filthy prison and rescued him, bringing him up with his own family – so successfully that he eventually became Mayor of Appleby.

Sizergh Castle is close by, the home of the Strickland family for twenty-seven generations. It too has a story of a locked room. In medieval times the fierce warrior-baron of the castle had a wife who he loved, yet deeply distrusted. When he was called away to war in Scotland he locked her in a room and told his servants not to release her on pain of death. This so frightened them that they chose to ignore the poor woman completely, leaving her to starve to death. Her ghost is said to haunt the castle screaming for release from a terrible captivity.

Sizergh Castle

One of the great eccentrics of the Lake District once lived at Castlehead, between Lindale and Grange-over-Sands. He was John 'Iron-Mad' Wilkinson who began here as an ironmaster and later invented many adventurous and innovative processes. He is credited with the building of the first iron boat, much to the consternation of the locals, who knew full well that iron would never float. At his death he was living at Bilston in Staffordshire, where he had built a chapel in cast-iron. Thus it was predictable that his will would dictate that he should be brought back for burial in the grounds of his beloved Castlehead (the estate where he had installed his mistress) in a cast-iron coffin.

The journey of the weighty cortège back to Cumbria must have been a nightmare – waggon, horses and coffin were almost abandoned in quicksands in Morecambe Bay – yet at last it reached Castlehead for the funeral. But then it was discovered that the will had stipulated inner shells for the coffin of lead and wood, and the original one was too small to accommodate these. A new coffin was constructed which proved to be too high for the grave, and this had to be dug deeper. A twenty-ton pyramid of iron was then erected over the grave and mourners and undertakers (who must have made a fortune from all this) departed from the scene. However within twenty years the Castlehead estate was sold and the new owners objected to the unusual mausoleum in the grounds. For a second time the great coffin was disinterred and a new burial-place was found for it in Lindale churchyard. Wilkinson's monument now stands just beyond the lodge of Castlehead. Its inscription reads:

John Wilkinson, Ironmaster, died July 14th, 1808, aged 80. His different works in various parts of the kingdom are lasting testimonies of his unceasing labours. His life was spent in action for the benefit of Man and, as he presumed, humbly, to hope, to the Glory of God. *Labore et Honore.*

The epitaph is somewhat at odds with his local reputation as an atheist (which may have had something to do with his disregard for local opinion in keeping a mistress at Castlehead), but at least he appears to have rested undisturbed at Lindale for the past 150 years, while his name lives on in the British steel industry. From 1907 until 1979 Castlehead was the home of the Holy Ghost Fathers, an order which sent missionaries to Africa, South America, and Pakistan.

Early in the Middle Ages the last wolf was killed in the Lake District. Some claim that this happened near Great Salkeld; others favour the sandy promontory of Humphrey Head, close to Grange. Here, it is said, the last wolf, which had been terrorising the district, was finally brought to bay by Sir John Harrington. He was the son of Sir Edgar Harrington, a powerful baron who lived at Wraysholme. Sir Edgar was also the guardian of a beautiful young girl called Adela whom John came to love. When he asked his father for permission to marry Adela, Sir Edgar was enraged and disinherited his son. John joined the Crusades, fought bravely on many occasions, and was knighted on the field of battle. After some years he returned secretly to his father's castle, where he found a great feast in progress. In the course of this Sir Edgar announced that should anyone be bold enough to kill the wolf that had been plundering Cartmel and its neighbourhood, he would bestow on that person the hand of Adela in marriage together with half of his estates. Thus, by slaying the wolf, Sir John was restored to his sweetheart, his family, and his fortune.

Another story of Cartmel which has a sounder basis in fact dates from January 1799 when a beggar was found on the nearby fells almost frozen to death. He was brought to Cartmel and revived with gin and tea. Although these beverages brought him back to consciousness, he only survived for a few days before succumbing to the exposure that he had suffered. The Upper Holker Township Book carries the account of what happened subsequently:

> ... after he died, on taking off his breeches – which he would never suffer to be taken off while alive – they felt very heavy; on examining them a bag was found in the Fob which contained One Hundred and Eighty-Five Guineas and a Half in gold which astonished us all present, all which it was supposed he had got by begging; he travelled the country with a certificate which he had somehow procured from St Thomas' Hospital, London, and pretended he had been cut for the stone and showed a small stone which he said was extracted from his Bladder. . . .

Since the son the beggar had named as his next of kin could not be found and there was no-one else with a claim on his wealth, land was bought with it which still yields benefit for the poor of Upper Holker through the Charity of the Beggar's Breeches.

One of the administrators of this charity was Mr Stockdale, author of *The Annals of Cartmel* and a well-respected local historian. In 1809 he sent his young servant boy out from Cark Hall with newspapers for the Cavendishes at Holker Hall. When the boy returned he was in a sorry state and fainted on the floor of the kitchen. Revived by an inhalation of burnt feathers and hartshorn, he gasped out that he had been chased by a dobbie all the way from Holker. The dobbie had been in the form of a ball of fire. The master and the other servants scoffed at the boy and told him to pull himself together (or suchlike, in the language of the day). But the story was remembered eight years later when a similar incident befell Mr Stockdale's brother. At first he thought the strange, bobbing light that he saw was the lantern of either a poacher or gamekeeper. When it grew closer he realised that it must be either a dobbie or the 'Going Fire' (the Will o' the Wisp or Jack o'Lantern of other parts). In earlier days, before the land was as well drained as it is today, it was comparatively common to witness this phenomenon, the spontaneously ignited marsh gas that dances along just above the ground on warm, still nights. Even so, it was generally believed that misfortune would befall those who saw it.

The ghost of a sad girl haunts a remote spot on Cartmel Fell. She mourns for her sweetheart, a charcoal burner, who was struck dead by lightning as he sat outside his hut. After this she was heartbroken, and refused to leave the stone he had been sitting on when the lightning struck. Friends brought her food which she would accept, but she hardly stirred from her seat, constantly crying his name. At last the cold of winter killed her, though the plaintive voice may still be heard calling the lover's name.

Kendal, the largest town in the old county of Westmorland, claims to be the Gateway to the Lakes. It is a pleasant place of interesting old buildings, a lot of them pubs. The name of the Angel Inn honours an earlier hostelry that stood close by today's building. The original Angel got its name from the occasion of Prince Charles Edward Stuart's visit to Kendal in 1745. Most citizens took cover from the fierce clansmen but inadvertently a small child was left playing on the floor of the inn after the rest of the family had hidden themselves. Just as angry Scots soldiers were about to seize the infant they were frightened away by an angel which gently guarded the abandoned child until the return of its parents.

An unusual relic in the parish church commemorates an earlier military episode in Kendal. The Philipson family who lived on Long Holme, later Belle Isle, on Lake Windermere were Royalist supporters during the Civil War. Robert Philipson became one of the most

Kendal Church

dashing of the Cavaliers, earning the nickname of 'Robin the Devil' for his fearless exploits. To his chagrin he had to take refuge on Long Holme while being pursued by Roundheads under the command of Colonel Briggs. He felt humiliated by this and vowed to take his revenge, expecting to confront the Colonel during Sunday service at Kendal. This account of the incident was printed in *The Folklore of the Lake District*:

> The next day being Sunday, Mr Robert Philipson with three or four more rode to Kendal to take revenge of the committee men. He passed the watch and rode into the church, up one aisle and down another to sacrifice; one of them met him, whom I shall not name, but he was dehorsed in his return by the guards, and his girths broke, but his partners relieved him by a desperate charge, and Robin in a trice clapped his saddle on horse-back and vaulted on him without girth or stirrup, killed a sentinel and galloped away returning to the island by two o'clock. Upon this and suchlike adventures he was commonly called 'Robin the Devil', but he was killed at last in the Irish wars at Washford fight as is reported.

31

In the mêlée, it seems, Robin dropped both his sword and his helmet, and today these may be seen hanging in the church near the Bellingham Chapel, though there is some doubt as to whether the sword is really the one flourished so dramatically by Philipson.

The Copper Kettle, a café in Widman St, Kendal, was haunted in 1981. The *Westmorland Gazette* reported that 'Ghostly Goings-on were Baffling New Proprietors'. The most unpleasant feature of the episode was the ghost apparently pushing one of the ladies who ran the café down the stairs having put out the lights first. She landed in a heap at the bottom of the stairs, and said that she could feel the imprint of its hands for at least two hours afterwards.

At Bleaze Hall, a farm close to the M6 at Old Hutton, a ghostly funeral makes a sombre procession. Apparently this is a re-enactment of the burial of a girl who died there seven centuries ago, heartbroken when her lover disappeared during a Crusade. Whether hers is the ghost that also troubles 'the haunted bedroom' is not known. Jessica Lofthouse wrote of sleeping in this room undisturbed. Bleaze Hall is one of the old Cumbrian houses which preserves a Dobbie stone to ward off evil spirits. These are usually three-faced prehistoric hammerheads, and are also supposed to have the power to return to their homes should they be taken away.

Kirkby Lonsdale, in the extreme east of the area, has a bridge built by the Devil overnight. This crosses the Lune, and the story has the Devil appearing to an old woman whose cow has managed to stray to the far side of the river, which soon afterwards rose in flood. (Another version says the bridge had to be built to allow her husband a safe return home from market: she was afraid that he would attempt to ford the swollen river and be drowned.) In return for the bridge the Devil claimed the soul of the first being to cross it.

All night the Devil roamed the countryside seeking stones with which to build his bridge. He had a mishap when he dropped an apronful of stones on Casterton Fell (where they can still be seen) but by dawn the bridge was complete and handsome. The conclusions of the story also differ. In the first version the woman throws a bun across the bridge and releases her small dog from her apron to cross the bridge to get it: in the second as soon as she sees her husband (the Devil's intended prey) approach she calls to the farm dog which has accompanied his master to market and flourishes a juicy bone so that the dog runs across the new bridge before her husband. In both instances the Devil is cheated of a human soul, and disappears with a

'The river soon afterwards rose in flood.'

howl of rage, leaving behind his neck-collar which can still be seen amongst the rocks downstream from the bridge. Other similar 'Devil's Bridge' stories are to be found in Wales, Yorkshire, and even Switzerland.

Grayrigg is a long way from Kirkby Lonsdale, being just six miles to the north-east of Kendal. The original Grayrigg Hall no longer stands, having suffered from 'the Quaker's Curse' uttered, in 1660 or thereabouts, by Francis Howgill. He was unjustly committed to Appleby gaol by Judge Duckett, who lived at Grayrigg Hall. Released from prison by means of a bond raised by fellow Quakers, Howgill made his way to Grayrigg and confronted the judge with a famous curse:

> I am come with a message from the Lord. Thou hast persecuted God's people – but God's hand is now against thee! Thy name shall rot out of the earth, and this house shall become desolate, a habitation for owls and jackdaws!

Howgill went on to become a famous Quaker preacher and suffered greatly for his faith, dying in prison in 1669. Judge Duckett's family also suffered, and by the end of the eighteenth century all the conditions of the curse had come to pass.

Finally Selside Hall, just off the A6 a short distance to the north of Kendal, used to have a particularly troublesome ghost in the old days before electricity. It would rush about the house extinguishing every lamp and candle. An extremely ancient yew tree in the grounds of the house was once used for hanging sheep-stealers: perhaps one of the victims sought revenge on the house where he suffered.

Chapter Three

# Around Windermere and Coniston

Newby Bridge is at the southern, lower, end of Lake Windermere. Before the bridge was built, travellers had to cross the River Leven, which takes the water of Windermere to the sea, by one of the two fords. The broader of these was Tinker's Ford, eighty yards wide but only a couple of feet or so deep, and perfectly safe as long as you avoided the 'bottomless' Dog Hole. The tinker who gave the name to the ford drowned here, standing helplessly upright and completely submerged, his heavy pack still on his back.

There is a strange story about the peaceful village of Finsthwaite close to Newby Bridge on the western shore of the lake. It is said that the illegitimate daughter of Prince Charles Edward Stuart was raised in a Catholic household here after her father's defeat at Culloden. In 1913 a white cross was put up in the churchyard to mark the resting-place of Clementina Johannes Sobieski Douglass, who came to the village in 1745, 'a princess', the villagers said, 'with wonderful fair hair' (Collingwood), and was buried here on 16 May 1771.

The name Sobieski derives from the Polish royal family: the Prince's mother was a Polish princess, while Douglas was the name he used when he was in hiding. The child's mother was almost certainly another Clementina, the daughter of John Walkenshawe, an aide to the Prince. She nursed the Prince during his illness after the Battle of Falkirk and became his mistress. She subsequently claimed that he had married her then.

It was always accepted at Finsthwaite that the princess, with two servants, arrived there in 1745, 'or thereabouts'. The mystery to me is whether the princess was the mother or the child. With the Prince's mother's family as a middle name it seems most likely to have been the latter, in which case she died at the tragically early age of twenty-six.

The lower reaches of Lake Windermere may lack the sheer spectacle of its northern end, but there is still a subtle quality to its scenery only slightly marred by the heavy traffic both on the lakeside highway and on the lake itself, especially at weekends. In winter the wind can blow

Waterhead, Windermere

down on the lake from the surrounding hills with sudden ferocity. Was it the sound of this unexpected icy blast, rattling twigs and moaning through branches, that gave rise to the story of the Wild Hunt or Hounds of Gabriel frequenting this end of the lake? Or might the weird moaning noises be caused by the release of pockets of air trapped beneath a blanket of ice, a phenomenon described by Wordsworth in *The Prelude*:

> *From under Esthwaite's splitting fields of ice*
> *The pent-up air, struggling to free itself,*
> *Gave out to meadow grounds and hills a loud*
> *Protracted yelling, like the noise of wolves*
> *Howling in troops along the Bothnic Main.*

About two miles up the east side of the lake from its southern end is the estate called Blakeholme Wray. An old stone hut stands by the lakeside here; it is believed to have been the shelter put up by a Spaniard, a fugitive from the Armada, who landed at Maryport. His name was Cornelius, and the hut is still known locally as Cornelius Shop.

A little further to the north, close to the Beech Hill Hotel, people were often troubled by a fierce boggle as they made their way to the ferry. As they disembarked near Graythwaite they were likely to meet an equally feersome malevolent spirit which seemed to favour Saturday nights for its hauntings. Hereabouts too there were tales of a phantom boat which sailed the lake on dark nights, 'with terrible sights aboard'.

The only ferry to cross Lake Windermere today is the car ferry that operates midway up the lakeside, crossing from the Ferry Inn on the eastern shore to the Nab, opposite. Formerly this was a humble row-boat, operated by ferrymen who lived in shoreside cottages or shelters. One stormy night an eery voice was heard calling for the ferry from the Nab, its sound carrying above the noise of wind and rain. While his colleagues chose to ignore this call, preferring the comforts of the inn, one intrepid ferryman set off across the lake to collect the late passenger. Some long time later he returned, ashen-faced. Utmost fear had struck him dumb, and the next day he died without being able to tell of the sight he had seen. This terrible spirit continued to be heard on wild nights by the ferrymen who had now learned to ignore its calls. At last, however, the calls became so persistent that a priest was called in to lay the ghost. He committed it to lie entombed in the quarry at Claife 'until dryshod men walk on Winander (Windermere) and trot their ponies through solid crags . . . as long as ivy should be green'. Even after the exorcism Claife was felt to be deeply spirit-ridden. On more than one occasion foxhounds stopped dead here after running in full cry and whimpered their refusal to continue the hunt.

What caused the original evil spirit to appear to the unfortunate ferryman? Was it an echo of one of the tragedies that occurred here in the seventeenth century? On 19 October 1635, forty-seven wedding-guests, returning home mellow after the ceremony, were drowned when the overladen ferry sank beneath them, and in the same month in 1681 'the great boat upon Windermere sunck about sunsetting – From sudden death *libera nos*'.

Another possibility may be that the Crier was the unhappy spirit of Thomas Lancaster who was born at High Wray on Windermere. In 1671 he cruelly murdered his wife, six of her family and a young servant at their home at Threlkeld, near Keswick. He poisoned them all with white arsenic which he also gave to several of his neighbours; fortunately none of the latter died in consequence. As was the custom,

'The Ferry, Winander Mere Lake'

he was taken back to his native county to suffer his punishment. He was hung from the doorpost of his birthplace at High Wray and then taken down and gibbeted at Sawrey Causeway, close to the road from the ferry. People swore that even after his remains were taken down from the gibbet and buried, his skeleton could still be seen (and heard) swinging in its iron cage.

The famous legend of the Skulls of Calgarth belongs to the upper reaches of Lake Windermere. Calgarth Hall stands by the lake near Troutbeck Bridge. It once belonged to the Philipson family, whose most notorious member, Robin the Devil, we met in the previous chapter riding into Kendal church in pursuit of an enemy. One account of the legend, dating from 1788, suggests that he was to blame for the skulls' persistent presence at Calgarth. In his *Survey of the Lakes* Clarke wrote that the two skulls at Calgarth

... were said to belong to persons whom Robin had murdered and that they could not be removed from the place where they then were; that when they were removed they always returned even though they had been thrown into

Regatta on Windermere

the Lake, with many other ridiculous falsehoods of the same stamp: some person has lately carried one of them to London and as it has not found its way back again, I shall say no more on so trivial a subject.

Clarke is alone in casting Robin the Devil as the villain of the piece. The most generally told version has Myles Philipson of Calgarth jealous of a piece of land held by neighbours, Kraster and Dorothy Cook. They refused to sell, but Myles overcame this by inviting them to a Christmas party at Calgarth, afterwards accusing them of stealing a valuable silver cup which was found concealed at their farm, planted there by the villainous landowner. The Cooks were brought to trial, found guilty, and hanged, but not before Dorothy had comprehensively cursed Calgarth and the family living there:

Guard thyself, Myles Philipson; thou thinkest thou hast managed grandly, but that tiny lump of land is the dearest a Philipson has ever bought or stole, for you will never prosper, neither your breed. Your schemes will wither, the side you take will lose, Philipsons will own no land, and while

Calgarth shall stand we will haunt it night and day. Never will you be rid of us.

The Philipsons built a new hall on the plot of land stolen from the unfortunate Cooks, but the terms of the curse came true. The splendid new house was constantly troubled by the ghostly skulls which could never be banished from the place. They were carried away, burnt, buried in quicklime, but each and every time they returned, the family all the time declining in wealth and status, constantly supporting losing sides. It is only fair to point out here that the legend might have been fabricated by the Cromwellians to discredit the Philipsons who were important Royalist sympathisers during the Civil War. However the story concludes that the haunting only came to an end when Bishop Watson of Llandaff bought the estate, exorcised the skulls and had them bricked up in a wall of the house. The bishop died in 1816, having spent thirty years in office and only once visiting his see, but nonetheless accepting the thousand pounds a year his office brought him. The exorcism of the skulls must have been a rare ecclesiastical duty! His neglect of his diocese came from an enduring love of his native county, and he was forever inventing grandiose schemes to improve his lands. One of these was to drain Lake Windermere. Fortunately, like most of his plans, this came to nothing. However he was, according to De Quincey, 'a joyous jovial and cordial host', and when Sir Walter Scott first visited the Lake District in 1805 he stayed at Calgarth with the Bishop. The story of the skulls would have appealed to his romantic nature even though Collingwood rather miserably remarks that 'we have enough romance in Lakeland, both ancient and modern, to afford the loss of one or two tales like this. . . . '

Another piece of Philipson land, given to them by Charles I, also had a strange history. It was a small tract of fell which supported a small farm that had once belonged to Hugh Hird, the Troutbeck Giant, who also liked to be called 'the Cork Lad of Kentmere'. Hird was supposed to have been the son of a monk from Furness Abbey. His mother, outcast from the district, wandered the countryside with her child, at last coming to Kentmere where they probably entered the service of the de Gilpins. This was in the reign of Edward VI when Kentmere Hall was in the process of being enlarged from the original pele tower to a larger residence, more suitable for a wealthy and influential family. Hugh was noticed for his prodigious feats of strength in helping to build the enlarged Hall. 'He lifted into its place

Bishop Watson of Llandaff

the mantle-tree of the kitchen fire-place, which ten men had in vain endeavoured to move' (Sullivan).

Soon afterwards it seems that Hugh and his mother left Kentmere to live in a derelict 'tenement' that belonged to the Crown. This he renovated, and when the rightful tenant appeared he defied him to enter, standing in the doorway so that it was completely blocked by his bulk. Indignantly the tenant complained to the King who summoned Hugh to explain himself in London.

Brought before the monarch the young giant demonstrated his fantastic strength in any number of ways and soon became a favourite of the court. When asked by King Edward what he ate to keep up his strength, he replied that he would have porridge and milk thick enough for a mouse to walk over for breakfast, and the sunny side of a wedder (sheep) for dinner. Challenged on this latter assertion, he proceeded to demonstrate that he could indeed finish off an entire sheep at a sitting. He was then called upon to take on the champion wrestler of southern England and, when he had successfully overcome his opponent, the King, forgetting Hugh's original defiance of the Crown, promised him any gift that he might reasonably bestow. Hugh

Kentmere Hall

42

chose to ask for rightful use of his humble 'tenement' during his lifetime, with a field of turf and a stand of timber for fuel (Hird's Wood is still to be seen on Ordnance Survey maps).

The gentle giant was employed in the district for his strength, moving great boulders single-handed and uprooting trees. It seems that it was the latter task that finally killed him, though he enjoyed possession of his smallholding for twenty-two years. After his death the property reverted to the Crown who passed it on to the Philipsons.

An alternative version of this legend, dating from 1692, maintains that Hird (or Heard, as it is spelt here) came to the King's notice through a notable feat of bravery. He single-handedly took on a party of Scots raiders, scattering them with the power and accuracy of his arrows. They retreated, believing that they had encountered a whole company of archers.

Reston House is a handsome Georgian mansion just to the east of the strangely-named village of Ings, on the road between Windermere and Kendal. It is supposed to have been built for Robert Bateman, a local lad who found his fortune as a marble merchant at Leghorne in Italy. In 1743, hearing that his new house was completed, he set out for home, sending before him a final consignment of marble intended for the floor of the church at Ings. Mystery surrounds the fate that befell him on his journey home. There is a story that the captain of his ship killed him near Gibraltar and threw his body into the sea, but he may have simply died either on the journey or before setting out. In any event, although his body never reached Reston House it seems that his spirit managed the long trip, for a ghost has often been seen restlessly watching at the gates of the property, though it never ventures inside the house. Local legend has it that Bateman was a confirmed batchelor, actively disliking women, and this accounts for the fact that no woman has been able to live in the place as owner or tenant for long.

Ghosts and smugglers often worked well together, frightening tales of the former often discouraging ordinary mortals from investigating strange lights and sounds too closely. The same may have been true of the other Duty Dodgers, the illicit whisky-makers who ran their secret stills in cottages, barns and quarries on remote fellsides.

The most famous of these unlawful characters was Lanty Slee who was able to offer an excellent product to those in the know for just ten shillings a gallon. Since some of Lanty's best customers were the local magistrates, he always received fair warning of any forthcoming raid, and usually managed to hide his equipment in time. He was one of the best-loved characters of the district in the latter half of the nineteenth century, and when for once his still was seized and stored overnight in the stables of the White Lion at Ambleside, in the morning the vital 'worm' was missing and, presumably, production of the local nectar recommenced.

One hiding-place for Lanty's still was by the shore of Red Tarn, a tiny mountain lake between Wrynose and Langdale. Jessica Lofthouse tells of a strange experience that happened to friends of hers who made their way up to the tarn from Wrynose Bottoms. All the way they followed a clear set of footprints set distinctly into new snow, yet at the tarn they simply ended. No-one was to be seen, nor was there a hole in the ice.

The following account appeared in the *Westmorland Gazette* on 21 September 1979:

> The mystery surrounding a ghostly figure which is haunting the grounds of a Lakeland Estate took a chilling turn this week.
>
> The spectral figure of a man has been seen several times in the past two years by the staff at the Langdale Outdoor Education Centre, Elterwater. And now an eery link has been found between the apparition and a man killed in an explosion at Elterwater over 60 years ago.
>
> The bearded man with a pockmarked face, wearing an old-fashioned collarless shirt and a flat leather cap has been seen walking through the grounds, in passageways and dormitories, and has appeared fleetingly at windows.
>
> Last week two schoolchildren who were staying at the centre told wardens they had been frightened by a strange man dressed in old clothes in the dining room.

The staff at the Langdale Centre had already investigated the history of the estate and found that the buildings occupied the site of a gunpowder factory which closed down in the 1920s. In September 1916 four men were killed in an explosion at the factory, one of them John Foxcroft, whose photograph was printed in the local newspaper after the disaster. When the children who had claimed to see the ghost were asked to draw the face of the man that they had seen, their efforts uncannily resembled the features of John Foxcroft printed in the *Westmorland Gazette*. Yet they had not known of the accident or seen the old newspaper. On another occasion one of the wardens sleeping in

'Bogies, kobolds, gnomes, and all manner of evil influences are in the very entrails of the Old Man.'

a hut on the site was woken by a strange old-fashioned figure who asked him: 'Is everything all right at home?'

In the middle years of the last century Mrs Lynn Linton wrote of the variety of bad spirits that lurked about the mineshafts and workings around Coniston. There were 'bogies, kobolds, gnomes and all manner of evil influences in the very entrails of the Old Man.'

Although it is a foot or so less in height than the Old Man of Coniston, Swirl How is hardly a less important mountain. It is the central peak of the group of mountains, and ridges radiate from it in every direction.

Climbers who begin their ascent of Swirl How from Coniston will soon be aware of Simon's Nick, in Wainwright's words: 'a remarkable cleft – a great vertical slice taken out of a high wall of rock'. This is an area where there was intense mining activity in days gone by, and between the Nick and Levens Water the landscape is scarred by an array of caves, shafts and potholes – all potentially lethal. It must have been here that Simon worked who gave his name to the Nick.

45

One day he struck a rich vein of copper and proudly told his rival miners that fairies had guided him to the lode (though the former were unconvinced and, knowing Simon's character, gave the Devil the credit). However even though Simon had now 'struck it rich' he failed to prosper. He was constantly robbed of his hard-won ore and accident followed accident. A final explosive mishap was the end of Simon, blown up by his own gunpowder. Since then the ghost of the old miner has occasionally appeared to climbers hanging precariously on the rock-face to which he gave his name.

A different sort of apparition was once observed and photographed by a young walker ascending Coniston Old Man by the Walna Scar path. His pictures of a flying saucer made the front page of the tabloids in 1954. Levens Water, between the Old Man and Swirl How, is supposed to contain a monstrous hairy trout, 'bigger than man had ever seen' while Goat's Water, which blocks direct access to the rock-climbers' favourite grounds on Dow Crag, is also well haunted. Here there are supposed to be giants, pygmies, and an assortment of evil fairies who spend their time terrifying the lone traveller with their wails and moans. The muddle of shapeless rocks below the rock face was said to have been the remains of their great city, ruined aeons ago. A.H. Griffin wrote of a strange experience here, in his book *In Mountain Lakeland*:

> I've also heard voices when climbing with a companion on Dow Crag although I've been certain that there was nobody else on the mountain. The voices seemed tantalisingly clear, but not quite near enough to distinguish the words, although we could sense the rise and fall of the sentences. We thought at first that we might be listening to the chattering of ravens, but not even ravens could sound as human as those voices.... They were far too lifelike to have been the wind whispering round the gullies, and I've often wondered whether it is possible for the wind to carry voices for a mile or two. I can't think of any other explanation.

In gloomy weather this whole area can seem oppressive. On the sides of the surrounding mountains are the wreckages of several aircraft that failed to clear the high ridges. Particularly unfortunate was the one that crashed near the summit of Great Carrs. Its undercarriage grounded and was ripped off a few feet below the ridge while the fuselage tumbled down the precipice on the other side.

Although the mineshafts and potholes of this area have claimed more victims than will ever be known for sure, it is possible to tell a story with a happier ending. In June 1921 a Londoner named Crump set out to walk from Coniston to Wasdale Head. Lost in mist, he fell twice, badly damaged his ankles, and ended up trapped in Piers Gill, the great chasm that divides Great End from Lingmell.

He must have been resigned to dying in that dark lonely cleft. Piers Gill had then only been climbed on two occasions, because the sheer volume of water tumbling down the pitches made it impossible except in the driest weather. But June 1921 was exceptionally dry, and because of this three climbers decided that it was time for them to try the first descent of the Gill. Imagine their astonishment when, halfway down the descent, they saw Mr Crump lying against a boulder, in the last stages of exhaustion. He had been there for twenty days and nights, and had long since finished his provisions – a small piece of gingerbread and a sandwich. Fortunately he had been able to find a trickle of water and the warm dry weather had enabled him to stay alive. Later he was able to revisit the scene of his accident.

Chapter Four

# Thirlmere

The road north from Windermere and Ambleside skirts Rydal Water and Grasmere before climbing to reach its summit – Dunmail Raise – and dropping down to Thirlmere.

William Wordsworth died at Rydal Mount, between Ambleside and Grasmere, in 1850, shortly after his eightieth birthday. In 1909 a Miss Ward, who was the daughter of the author of *Recollections*, an early book on supernatural experiences, wrote of staying there. She occupied a first-floor corner room, above the small sitting-room and, perhaps for the benefit of her mother, wrote of her experiences:

William Wordsworth

The blind was half up, the window wide open, the curtain drawn aside over the back of a wooden armchair that stood against the window. A moonlight night.

I slept soundly, but woke quite suddenly, at what hour I do not know, and found myself sitting bolt upright in bed looking towards the window. Very bright moonlight was shining into the room, and I could just see the corner of Loughrigg in the distance...

Then I suddenly became conscious of the moonlight striking on something, and I saw perfectly clearly the figure of an old man sitting in the armchair beside the window. I said to myself, 'That's Wordsworth!' He was sitting with either hand resting on the arms of the chair, leaning back, his head rather bent, and he seemed to be looking down, straight in front of him, with a rapt expression. He was not looking at me or out of the window. The moonlight lit the top of his head, and the silvery hair, and I noticed that the hair was very thin.

The whole impression was of something solemn and beautiful, and I was not in the least frightened.

At last she had to move, and as she did so the figure melted away so that all she could see was the chair. The next day she learned that she had been sleeping in Dorothy Wordsworth's room.

Dunmail Raise is said to take its name from Domhnall, the son of Owain, last of the Celtic kings of Cumbria. In 945 King Edmund, who ruled almost undisputed over the remainder of England, joined his forces with those of King Malcolm of Scotland in order to defeat the last bastion of Celtic resistance in his kingdom which continued to defy him from the mountain fastnesses of Cumbria. In the last great battle Domhnall was defeated, his body carried away from the field by faithful warriors and buried under a great pile of stones on the Raise, as he had instructed. His golden crown was thrown into Grisedale Tarn, again on his wishes, as the warriors fled eastwards. Legend has it that the crown was enchanted, giving its wearer a magic right to the kingdom — thus it was vitally important to prevent it from falling into Saxon hands. Each year Domhnall's warriors return to the tarn to make sure that the crown still rests there. They carry it back to the grave of their chief and each strikes the stones of the monument with their spear-butt. At this Domhnall stirs, and his voice comes from the grave: 'Not yet, not yet, the time has not yet come. Wait awhile.' On hearing these words the warriors turn back to the tarn with the crown, and restore it to its dark resting-place.

Domhnall is also seen here pursuing a fair female ghost to whom he was said to have been betrothed. Both figures eventually disappear into the mist which so frequently veils the fellside.

King Edmund ruthlessly crushed all remaining resistance in the kingdom, putting out the eyes of Domhnall's two surviving sons to prevent them from leading any further rebellion. If Domhnall was already married, with two sons, his persual of the young maiden seems unlikely, especially as history asserts that the Celtic king was successful in escaping from the Saxons, dying later when on pilgrimage to Rome. Many of the Cumbrians who were captured at this time were transported to North Wales where they were notorious for their red hair, lawless behaviour, and reckless love of women. They were probably the forebears of the Red Brigands of South Gwynedd who were cruelly suppressed in the sixteenth century, their coppery hair making them distinct from the native tribes.

Grisedale Tarn lies below the summit of Seat Sandal, a peak described by A.H. Griffin as 'a mountain of ghosts'. He tells of an incident experienced by an Ulverston lady and her friend as they climbed towards the summit from the tarn:

Ahead of them, but always just out of sight, they could hear two men talking, and from time to time they could hear a dog barking. All the way up the steep grassy slope they could hear the men and their dog just ahead, and keeping their distance, and they fully expected to see them at any moment. But when they reached the summit and could see for miles around and all the way down the other side, there was just no-one there. The men − and the dog − had vanished in the mountain air.
(The Roof of England.)

Grisedale Tarn was the scene of Wordsworth's last farewell to his brother John, who perished in the wreck of the *Earl of Abergavenny* off Portland in February 1805. A stone, called the Brothers' Stone, stands by the tarn bearing lines composed by the poet in memory of his brother:

> *− Brother and friend, if verse of mine*
> *Have power to make thy virtues known*
> *Here let a monumental Stone*
> *Stand − sacred as a Shrine;*
> *And to the few who pass this way,*
> *Traveller or Shepherd, let it say,*

*Long as these mighty rocks endure, –*
*Oh do not thou too fondly brood,*
*Although deserving of all good,*
*On any earthly hope, however pure!*

Two other small tarns in this district may also have supernatural visitors. Both lie to the west of Dunmail, below the summit of High Raise. Easedale Tarn, 'a gem in a wild setting', is easily reached from Grasmere. Wordsworth disliked Easedale, calling it 'the black quarter' since it was from this direction that bad weather usually came. A lost soul is said to dwell in the waters of the tarn, searching for its rightful place in the world of spirits but never finding it, and wailing its unhappiness.

Codale Tarn lies even higher, a puddle of a tarn on a ledge above a cove. This too has its lost soul, while its waters are said to be able to reflect the faces of the dead.

Before 1890 there were just two small lakes occupying the lovely valley that Thirlmere covers today. Wordsworth would have been

Thirlmere Bridge, looking north

51

horrified by the transformation wrought by Manchester Corporation when they flooded the valley to create the reservoir. A favourite outing enjoyed by the poet was to an inn where he would meet with Coleridge. This disappeared in 1894 beneath the waters dammed for the benefit of the citizens and industry of Manchester. Armboth House vanished at the same time, and only its distinctive Monkey Puzzle tree survives by the lakeside car park to serve as a reminder of a place that was once famous for its ghosts.

Harriet Martineau appears to have been the first writer to mention the spectacular hauntings at Armboth when she wrote in her *Guide to the English Lakes*, published in 1855:

> ... Lights at night, bells ring, and as all are set off ringing a large black dog — a ghost hound? — is seen swimming across the lake. Plates and dishes clatter, and a table is spread by unseen hands preparing for a ghostly wedding feast of a murdered bride about to rise from her watery grave to keep her terrible nuptials.... There is something remarkable, like witchery, about the house.

These busy apparitions were supposed only to appear on the night of Hallowe'en when they would join with other ghosts of the neighbourhood (including the Skulls of Calgarth) in a night of debauched revelry.

As in very many other instances, a simple tale of a betrayed bride has suffered from the additions and embellishments of a hundred fireside storytellers. In this case the worst damage was probably inflicted by the verse of Alexander Craig Gibson, who introduced the idea of a gathering of ghosts visiting Armboth on Hallowe'en. Gibson's poem is, however, written with tongue firmly in cheek, and reads all the better for that. As he died in 1874 he most probably borrowed the details of the Armboth haunting from Harriet Martineau.

W.T. Palmer, writing in 1905, joined Martineau's account with Gibson's verse to produce this version:

> Armboth House is the haunt of the grisliest set of phantoms the Lake Country holds. For once a year, on All Hallowe'en, it is said the ghosts of the Lake Country, the fugitive spirits whose bodies were destroyed in unavenged crime come here. Bodies without heads, the skulls of Calgarth with no bodies, a phantom arm which possesses no other member, and many a weird shape beside. But they are a moral lot of victims and not sinners. Does the wild shriek in which ere dawning ends their banquet

mean that to the spirit eyes has come a revelation of their wrongers in torment? But I forget; no man can hear that cry and live. Yet people will not believe the straightforward story of the Armboth ghosts, of windows lit up with corpse-lights, of clanking chains in corridors, of eternal shriekings which cannot be traced, as though murder was being done in some secret chamber. But why has this house been compelled to be a ghosts' haunt? I have never heard a word against its reputation, ancient or modern. Perhaps it is most central for guests to the ghost supper.
(From *The English Lakes.*)

The Castle Rock of Triermain is at the northern end of Thirlmere, a precipitous slab which was chosen by Sir Walter Scott as the romantic backcloth for his *Bridal of Triermain*:

> ... *midmost of the vale, a mound*
> *Arose, with airy turrets crown'd,*
> *Buttress, and rampire's circling bound,*
> *And mighty keep and tower* ...

'Castle Rock, resembling the archetypal Gothic castle of horror films.'

This was the scene that King Arthur's gaze fell on as he emerged from the narrow valley of St John. He enters the enchanted castle and meets the beautiful witch Guendolen, who 'beguiles' him through the night. In the morning he rides out from the enchanted castle, away from the witch's wicked influence, but she runs after him, beseeching him to at least take a last drink with her, so that they might part 'like lover and like friend'. As the King bent from his saddle to reach the goblet that she offered, a drop of the magic potion fell on his horse, which immediately sprang twenty feet into the air, sending the goblet flying:

> *The peasant still can show the dint*
> *Where his hoofs lighted on the flint.*
> *From Arthur's hand the goblet flew,*
> *Scattering a shower of fiery dew,*
> *That burned and blighted where it fell!*
> *The frantic steed rush'd up the dell,*
> *As whistles from the bow the reed;*
> *Nor bit nor rein could check his speed*
>    *Until he gain'd the hill;*
> *Then breath and sinew fail'd apace,*
> *And, reeling from the desperate race,*
>    *He stood, exhausted, still.*
> *The Monarch, breathless and amazed,*
> *Back on the fatal castle gazed:*
> *Nor tower nor donjon could he spy;*
> *Darkening against the morning sky;*
> *But, on the spot where once they frown'd,*
> *The lonely streamlet brawl'd around*
> *A tufted knoll, where dimly shone*
> *Fragments of rock and rifted stone....*
> *Know, too, that when a pilgrim strays,*
> *In morning mist or evening maze,*
>    *Along the mountain lone,*
> *That fairy fortress often mocks*
> *His gaze upon the castled rocks*
>    *Of the Valley of Saint John....*

The north face of the crag, with its horrendous overhang, was only conquered in 1939, by Jim Birkett, the quarryman from Little

Langdale, who was one of the pioneers of rock-climbing in the Lake District. Some of the most difficult pitches in Lakeland belong to this crag, not made any easier by spectators on the main road far below having a grandstand view of any embarrassments. Another less obvious drawback is its reputation for being haunted. Maybe it is the Rock's close-up resemblance to the archetypal Gothic castle of horror films that accounts for this, though there are some local climbers who believe that there is a more sinister and powerful force here that can cause toes suddenly to lose adhesion, or muscles to seize up with unexpected spasms of cramp. As William Hutchinson wrote in one of the earliest guidebooks to the Lake District:

– In the widest part of the dale you are struck with the appearance of an ancient ruined castle, which seems to stand upon the summit of a little mount, the mountain around forming an amphitheatre. This massive bulwark shews a front of various towers, and makes an awful, rude, and gothic appearance, with its lofty turrets, and ragged battlements; we traced the galleries, the bending arches, the buttresses; the greatest antiquity stands characterized in its architecture; the inhabitants near it assert it is an antediluvian structure.

The traveller's curiosity is rouzed, and he prepares to make a nearer approach, when that curiosity is put upon the rack, by his being assured, that if he advances, certain genii who govern the place, by virtue of their supernatural arts and necromancy, will strip it of all its beauties, and by inchantment transform the magic walls. The vale seems adapted for the habitation of such beings; its gloomy recesses and retirements look like haunts of evil spirits; there was no delusion in this report, we were soon convinced of its truth; for this piece of antiquity, so venerable and noble in its aspect, as we drew near, changed its figure, and proved no other than a shaken massive pile of rocks, which stand in the midst of this little vale, disunited from the adjoining mountains; and have so much the real form and resemblance of a castle, that they bear the name of THE CASTLE ROCKS OF ST JOHN'S. *(Author's note: Hutchinson was writing in the final years of the eighteenth century, long before Scott wrote* The Bridal of Triermain *which gave The Castle Rocks their alternative name.)*

As Collingwood explains in *The Lake Counties*, most of the mountains of Lakeland have a back and a front. From Thirlmere it is the backside of Helvellyn that is seen, its grassy and gentle slopes rather than its precipitous crags. From here there is no hint of the drama of its two razor-like ridges, Swirral Edge and Striding Edge.

55

Thirlmere and Helvellyn from Raven Crag

At the summit of Helvellyn there is a monument commemorating an accident that occurred on Striding Edge in 1803, when Charles Gough fell and was killed while on a walk with his dog. His body lay undiscovered for three months, and when it was found his faithful dog sat close by, still guarding him. Like Greyfriars' Bobby, Gough's dog Foxey soon became a national celebrity, both Wordsworth and Scott visiting the scene of the accident. Each poet composed poignant lines on the devotion of the little yellow terrier. Scott wrote:

> *How long didst thou think that his silence was slumber?*
> *When the wind waved his garment how oft didst thou start?*

Canon Rawnsley had the memorial erected in 1890, perhaps hoping to quench for all time the suspicion that the only way that the dog could have survived for so long was by taking sly bites out of the body of his late master.

Clark's Lowp was a prominent rock which overlooked the old Thirlmere (Leathe's Water) before inundation. 'Lowp' is the dialect form of 'Leap', and the story goes that there was once a man named

Clark who suffered so much from his scold of a wife that he at last decided to do away with himself. When he told his wife this she asked him what means he would use to bring his life to an end. 'I will hang myself,' he replied. 'Better not,' she said, 'for it is a painful death.'

'Then I will take my gun and shoot myself.'

'But you are such a poor shot that you will surely miss, or else injure yourself so that you will linger in agony.'

'Then I will make an end of it by drowning,' and so saying he took himself down to the lakeside, followed by his less than doting wife. As he prepared to wade out to the deep water she stopped him, begging him to jump into the lake instead from the overhanging rock to which he would give his name. Otherwise, she said, he would suffer needlessly from the cold water.

The couple then climbed up to the top of the crag. The wife advised him to take a good run before jumping, to avoid falling onto the rocks below. Clark followed her advice, landed in the deep water, and was soon drowned. Whereupon the wife, satisfied that she had behaved honourably by giving him such good advice, returned home in good humour.

Dalehead Hall, on the eastern side of Thirlmere almost opposite Armboth, was situated high enough to avoid the inundation which brought an end to the ghosts of Armboth. John Richardson, a mid-nineteenth-century schoolmaster who liked to write in dialect, once told of the boggle who haunted the Park here. Here the account is translated (!) into English:

Aye, I've seen the Park boggle different times, and the Armboth boggle too, not that I've minded them much. There's nothing to be afraid of, for they've never hurt anyone at all that I've heard tell of. I once spoke to the Park boggle, but it gave me no answer, and I'll tell you how it happened.

We'd had the hogs (the previous year's lambs) wintering down below Hawkshead. I'd been fetching them back, and as its a fair way, and I've a few acquaintances over that way, it took me a longish time and it was rather dark before I got to the Park. As I'd just got to the top, and was beginning to come down on this side, the sheep stopped in the middle of the road and wouldn't go a foot further. What! I shooed the dog up to help me on with them, but it wouldn't bark or anything, but kept creeping against my legs, like as if it was half frightened to death. I began to look then for what was frightening both the sheep and the dog, and sure enough I saw right in front of them what looked like a great heap of lime and soil which reached right

across the road. It went right up to the top of the bank on one side of the lane and sloped right down to about half a yard high on the other. Now I was sure that nobody would put a pile of muck across the road in that way, and was sure that it must be the Park boggle. I stood a little bit considering what to do, then I asked it what was the reason why the sheep should go no further. Just then one of them leaped right over the lower end of the heap, and then they all followed it helter-skelter down the road. When they were all over it I went up to it, and thought I would set my foot on it to see what it was; but when I should have stepped on it there was nothing there. It was gone altogether.

There was another time, too, that I saw the Park boggle, in another form; but I wasn't sure about it that time as I had been when I'd been fetching the hogs. I'd been walling a gap that had fallen over on the other side of the Park, and as the days were short, worked on until dusk. Then I happened to notice that some sheep had got themselves into an intake (walled enclosure) up on the fellside, and I thought that I'd better go up and get them out, and perhaps stop the gap with a bit of thorn. So I climbed up and by the time I'd got the sheep out and stopped the gap it was pitch dark. When I got to coming down again, I saw such a fire on the top of the Park as I'd never seen before in my life. It rose up to such a height, and sparks fell in showers

to all sides of it! What! I thought that it was very queer that anyone should kindle such a fire up there, so I decided I would go up and see what it meant. But when I got to the place, there was neither a fire nor any place where one had been! There was neither a black place, or gorse smouldering, or anything that I could see, but it wasn't a quarter of an hour since I'd seen a great fire blazing away furiously. No, you may make what you will of it, you may believe me or not, just as you like, but nobody will ever persuade me but that it was the Park boggle that I saw both times.

Chapter Five

# Keswick and the Central Fells

Threlkeld, at the northern end of the Vale of St John's, was the scene of one of the most horrible crimes ever perpetrated in Lakeland: in 1671 Thomas Armstrong poisoned his wife and six of her family here, and was later hung for their murders at High Wray, near Ambleside (*see* Chapter Three). Threlkeld Place had a legend of an indestructible skull similar to that of Calgarth. A tenant farmer who took on the property found that the previous tenant had left one small room locked and unused. Eventually he had the room opened up and was surprised to find a skull occupying a niche in the wall. The skull was removed and buried with reverence, but soon afterwards the farmer's wife,

The Vale of St John: Saddleback in the distance

going to the room to clean it, found the skull back in its niche. Not surprisingly, the farmer was startled by this and resolved to get rid of the skull once and for all. He took it to St Bee's Head and threw it as far as he could out to sea. The skull was back at Threlkeld before him, grinning from its niche.

Several more attempts were made to rid the house of the skull, but all were unsuccessful. At last the farmer admitted defeat and bricked it up in its niche. Soon afterwards he moved on to another farm in the neighbourhood leaving the skull in its original place. It appears not to have troubled the household since.

The towering, shattered, slopes of Blencathra (or Saddleback) rear up behind Threlkeld. Wainwright calls this:

> ... one of the grandest mountains in Lakeland and the most imposing of all.... There is nothing inviting in these shattered cliffs and petrified rivers of stone that seem to hold a perpetual threat over the community of Threlkeld and the surrounding countryside: the scene is awesome, intimidating and repelling. Few who gaze upon these desolate heights that leap so dramatically into the sky are likely to feel any inclination to venture into their arid, stony wildernesses and scramble up to the serrated summit ridge so high above.

However it turns out that to climb Blencathra's awesome southern face is one of the great enthusiast's favourite excursions, and it is one of the eighteen featured walks in *Fellwalking with Wainwright*. Hidden amongst 'these shattered cliffs and petrified rivers of stone' are two tarns, about two miles apart. The early tourists ascribed supernatural features to both of these lakelets.

Scales Tarn was said to be bottomless, a place where the sun's rays seldom penetrated, so that if you gazed into its surface at midday you would see the stars reflected in its waters. To quote from *The Bridal of Triermain* once more:

> *Though never sunbeam could discern*
> *The surface of that sable tarn,*
> *In whose black mirror you may spy*
> *The stars, while noontide lights the sky....*

Wainwright pours cold water on this by remarking that he has sat in warm sunshine by the tarn and has never seen the stars reflected on its waters in daylight. More interesting are the lava deposits in the vicinity. William Hutchinson, writing in the latter years of the eighteenth century, ascribed the phenomenon to Blencathra's other tarn, Bouscale (now Bowscale) Tarn:

Several of the most credible inhabitants thereabouts affirming, that they frequently see the stars in it at midday; but, in order to discover that phenomenon, the firmament must be perfectly clear, the air stable, and the water unagitated. These circumstances not occurring at the time I was there, deprived me of the pleasure of that sight, and of recommending it to the naturalists upon my own ocular evidence, which I regret the want of, as I question if the like has been any where else observed. The spectator must be situated at least 200 yards above the lake, and as much below the summit of the semi-ambient ridge; and, as there are other high mountains, which, in that position, may break and deaden the solar rays, I can only give an implicit credit to the power of their agency, till I am convinced of their effects, and am qualified to send it better recommended to the public.

It is difficult to understand how Hutchinson could have confused the two tarns, for Bowscale is not closely overshadowed by precipitous crags like Scales Tarn, though it is no less beautiful for that. However Bowscale also had its own legend, of two immortal fish, mentioned by Wordsworth in his *Song at the Feast of Brougham Castle*, which celebrated the escape of the 'Shepherd Lord' (the young Lord Clifford) during the Wars of the Roses:

> *– Again he wanders forth at will,*
> *And tends a flock from hill to hill:*
> *His garb is humble; ne'er was seen*
> *Such garb with such a noble mien....*
> *The eagle, lord of land and sea,*
> *Stooped down to pay him fealty;*
> *And both the undying fish that swim*
> *Through Bowscale-tarn did wait on him;*
> *The pair were servants of his eye*
> *In their immortality;*
> *And glancing, gleaming, dark or bright,*
> *Moved to and fro, for his delight.*

Wainwright, in Book Five of his *Pictorial Guide to the Lake District Fells* (The Northern Fells), points out that an excursion to Bowscale Tarn formed an essential part of the itinerary of the first tourists in

'... a Phantom Army was seen, on several occasions, to march along its ridge'

Lakeland who sought 'the picturesque'. Now, says Wainwright, the path to the tarn is neglected, but those early visitors were surely right – 'The setting *is* wild and romantic and *very* impressive; and Bowscale Tarn, in 1961 as in 1861, is one of the best scenes of its kind in the district.'

Souther Fell is an outlier to Blencathra, and the Victorians often began their ascent of the latter by using the gently-graded path leading across the slopes of Souther. The fell itself is a dull affair and the climb up to the summit unexciting, but it makes up for this by being a wonderful viewpoint, especially eastwards to the Pennines. However its main claim to fame dates back 250 years, when a Phantom Army was seen, on several occasions, to march along its ridge. This is the most famous of all the ghost stories of the Lake District, and its importance is such that it seems worthwhile to print the original account in full. This first appeared in the second volume of the *Lonsdale Magazine* in 1749 but is taken here from William Hutchinson's *The History of the County of Cumberland*, published in 1793–6. His book incorporated (or borrowed) the work of many other writers. In this case the author was George Smith, who made several

journeys into the nether regions of the Lake District in the middle
years of the eighteenth century. He wrote:

... Souter-fell *(Smith, or Hutchinson, preferred to spell Souther as it is
spoken)* is a distinguished mountain of itself where the astonishing
phenomenon appeared to exhibit itself, which, in 1735, 1737, and 1745,
made so much noise in the north, that I went on purpose to examine the
spectators, who asserted the fact, and continue in their assertion very
positively to this day.

On Midsummer eve, 1735, William Lancaster's servant related, that he
saw the east side of Souter-fell, towards the top, covered with a regular
marching army for above an hour together; he said they consisted of distinct
bodies of troops, which appeared to proceed from an eminence in the north
end, and marched over a niche in the top ... but, as no other person in the
neighbourhood had seen the like, he was discredited and laughed at. Two
years after, on Midsummer eve also, betwixt the hours of eight and nine,
William Lancaster himself imagined that several gentlemen were following
their horses at a distance, as if they had been hunting, and taking them for
such, he paid no regard to it, till about ten minutes after, again turning his
head towards the place, they appeared to be mounted, and a vast army
following, five in rank, crowding over at the same place where the servant
said he saw them two years before. He then called his family, who all agreed
in the same opinion; and, what was most extraordinary, he frequently
observed that some one of the five would quit rank, and seem to stand in a
fronting posture, as if he was observing and regulating the order of their
march, or taking account of their numbers, and, after some time, appeared
to return full gallop to the station that he had left, which they never failed to
do as often as they quitted their lines; and the figure that did so was
generally one of the middlemost men in the rank. As it grew later, they
seemed regardless of discipline, and rather had the appearance of people
riding from a market, than an army; though they continued crowding on,
and marching off, so long as they had light to see them.

This phaenomenon was no more seen till the Midsummer eve which
preceded the rebellion *(that of 1745)*, when they were determined to call
more families to be witness of this sight, and accordingly went to Wilton-
hill and Souter-fell side, till they convened about 26 persons, who all affirm
they then saw the same appearance, but not conducted with the usual
regularity as the preceding ones, having the likeness of carriages
interspersed; however, it did not appear to be less real; for some of the
company were so affected with it, as, in the morning, to climb the

mountain, through an idle expectation of finding horse shoes after so numerous an army; but saw not the vestige or print of a foot.

William Lancaster, indeed, told me that he never concluded they were real beings, because of the impractability of a march over the precipices where they seemed to come on; that the night was extremely serene; that horse and man, upon strict looking at, appeared to be but one being, rather than two distinct ones; that they were nothing like any clouds or vapours which he had ever perceived elsewhere; that their number was incredible, for they filled lengthways near half a mile, and continued so in a swift march for above an hour, and much longer, he thinks, if night had kept off. The whole story has so much the air of romance, that it seemed fitter for *Amedis de Gaul* or *Glenville's System of Witches*, than the repository of the learned; but as the country was full of it, I only give it verbatim from the original relation of a people that could have no end in imposing on their fellow creatures, and are of good repute in the place where they live.

It is my real opinion that they apprehended they saw such appearances; but how an undulating lambient meteor could affect the optics of many people is difficult to say. No doubt fancy will extend to miraculous heights in persons disposed to indulge it; and whether there might not be a concurrence of that to assist the vapour, I will not dispute. . . . Those who treat it as a mere illusion should assign reasons for so large a fascination in above 20 persons; probably one, indeed, might serve to aggrandise the fancy of others; but I should think they could not be so universally deceived without some stamina of the likeness exhibited on the mountain from a meteor or from some unknown cause.

Armistead, in *Tales of the English Lakes*, quotes the editor of the *Lonsdale Magazine*, saying that it was afterwards discovered that the rebel army was exercising on the western coast of Scotland at this time whose movements were reflected 'by some fine transparent vapour similar to the Fata Morgana'.

Furthermore, Hutchinson added an interesting postscript to the description of the incidents in *The History of Cumberland* by saying that 'Mr Clarke has corroborated the circumstances of this account, by adding, that Daniel Stricket, who first observed the spectacle (*i.e. William Lancaster's servant*), at the time of Mr Clarke's publishing, lived under Skiddaw, and was an auctioneer.' The cynical might say that anyone in this line of business must be able to exaggerate anything. Mr Clarke was a clergyman, the Rev. C.C. Clarke, who had visited Souther Fell in 1785 and included 'The Ghost Army' in his book *One Hundred Wonders of the World*. He had also taken the trouble to interview surviving witnesses of the event, getting them to sign an affidavit which said: 'We whose names are hereunto subscribed, declare that the above account be true, and that we saw the phaenomenon as here related. As witness our hands, this 21st day of July, 1785.'

Perhaps the sensation-seeking clergyman bullied the locals into signing, pointing out that they could hardly dilute their account at this time, forty years on, when the Ghost Army was already a legend. Needless to say, over the years that followed the story suffered embellishment. In 1855 Harriet Martineau wrote:

This Souter or Soutra Fell is the mountain on which ghosts appeared in myriads, at intervals during ten years of the last century; presenting the same appearances to twenty-six chosen witnesses, and to all the inhabitants of all the cottages within view of the mountain, and for a space of two hours and a half at one time – the spectral show being closed by darkness!

There are a few other accounts of ghostly armies in British ghostlore, and that of Souther Fell is not even unique in appearing in daylight. A famous description from the early Middle Ages concerns the Welsh Marches and is by a contemporary writer named Walter Map (this is quoted in Anthony Masters' book, *The Natural History of the Vampire*):

In Brittany there used to be seen at night long trains of soldiers who passed by in dead silence conducting carriages of booty, and from these the Breton peasants have actually stolen away horses and cattle and kept them for their own use. In some cases no harm seems to have resulted, but in other instances this was speedily followed by sudden death. Companies of these troops of night-wanderers, who are commonly called *Herlethingi*, were very well known in England even to the present day, the reign of our King Henry II, who is now ruling over us. These armies went to and fro without let or stay, hurrying hither and thither rambling about in the most mad vagrancy, all inceding in unbroken silence, and amongst the band there appeared alive many who were known to have been long since dead. This company of *Herlethingi* last espied in the Marches of Hereford and Wales in the first year of King Henry II, tramping along at high noon with carts and beasts of burden, with pack saddles and provender baskets, with birds and dogs and a mixed multitude of men and women. Those who first caught sight of this troop by their shouting and blowing of horns and trumpets aroused the whole district, and as in the manner of those border folk, who are ever on the watch, almost instantly there assembled various bands fully equipped, and because they were unable to obtain a word in reply from this strange host they incontinently prepared to make them answer to a shower of darts and javelins, and then the troop seemed to mingle with the air and forthwith vanish away out of sight. From that day this mysterious company has never been seen by man.

A 'phantom army of the sky' is supposed to have presaged the battle at Culloden that took place in the same year as the sighting at Souther Fell, and another was seen from Helvellyn on the eve of the Battle of Marston Moor, while in *Lark Rise to Candleford* Flora Thompson told of a ghost army that had been seen in Oxfordshire:

Some years before, the people in the hamlet had seen a regiment of soldiers marching in the sky, all complete with drum and fife band. Upon inquiry it had been found that such a regiment had been passing at the time along a road near Bicester, six miles away, and it was concluded that the apparition in the sky must have been a freak reflection.

An even more remarkable event was witnessed on Christmas Eve 1642, at Edge Hill near Stratford-upon-Avon. This was a re-enactment of the battle that had taken place there in the previous October when Royalists under Prince Rupert had met with the Roundhead forces. After a day's savage fighting, honours were about even, but one thousand troops were slain in the encounter. On Christmas Eve, between midnight and one in the morning, a party of shepherds and other country people were amazed to find themselves in the thick of the fight. The full horrifying sound of the battle surrounded them; they were even able to hear the groans of the dying and injured. It was easy to identify the participants by the colours they carried and the armour they wore − there was no question but that this was the Battle of Edge Hill being fought for a second time!

When the frightened country-folk returned to their village and told of their harrowing experience, it was decided to hold a vigil at the same spot on the following (Christmas) night. Again the dreadful sights and sounds were witnessed, and on subsequent occasions local worthies were persuaded to join the vigil. Their reports of the haunted battlefield reached the King, then at Oxford, and he appointed a commission to investigate the incident. It is unusual for a haunting to continue so long as to become almost predictable, but in this instance

the commission were able to report to the King that '. . . they saw the aforementioned prodigies, distinctly knowing divers of the apparitions, or incorporeal substances, by their faces, as that of Sir Edmund Varney and others that were slain. . . .'

The last illustration of a phenomenon which has more close parallels than might at first be expected, comes from modern times. A.H. Griffin retells an experience that happened to the late F.S. Smythe, mountaineer and writer, while he was climbing the Finsteraarhorn in the Alps:

> . . . He and his companion both saw what appeared to be a line of ships floating over the Black Forest. They looked like battle-cruisers and the two climbers could see every detail of the masts and funnels. For a quarter of an hour they watched this strange, heavenly Armada and then it disappeared. An interesting correspondence followed in *The Times*. It was suggested, for instance, that the ships had been taking part in exercises somewhere near the junction of the English Channel with the North Sea and that the image had been magnified, as well as refracted, by different layers of air – over a distance of something like 400 miles. An unconvincing explanation.
> (From *In Mountain Lakeland*.)

By way of an apology for this digression away from the Lakes, it is only right to conclude with Wordsworth's account of the haunting of Souter Fell:

> *Silent the visionary warriors go,*
> *Wending in ordered pomp their upward way,*
> *Till the last banner of the long array*
> *Had disappeared, and every trace is fled*
> *Of splendour – save the beacon's spiry head,*
> *Tipt with eve's latest gleam of burning red.*

There are wonderful views to be had from the summit of Walla Crag, which overlooks the eastern shore of Derwent Water. It is a pleasant half-day hike to climb to this summit, the perfect introduction to fell-walking, as Wainwright remarks. A hazard to avoid in its descent, however, is the precipitous gully known as Lady's Rake. This is said to have been named after the feat of the last Lady Derwentwater who, confined to her house on Lord's Island, having supported the Stuart cause, escaped with the family's treasures. Pursued by her captors, she managed to elude them by climbing this unlikely route.

Derwentwater from the entrance to Borrowdale

Sadly it was to no avail, for she had intended to use her wealth to buy the release of her husband who was awaiting execution in the Tower of London for high treason. Despite her intervention, he was executed in 1715. A few nights after his death there was a fantastic display of aurora borealis in the sky over Keswick, and this colourful phenomenon afterwards became known here as 'Lord Derwentwater's Lights'.

St Herbert's Island lies to the south of Lord's Island and is smaller. The saint who lived here in the seventh century was a devout, solitary man. He lived on fish from the lake and vegetables that he grew himself, spending the greater part of his time in devotions. This is a part of the world which seems to attract the recluse (and there have been several eccentric hermits living hereabouts in this century): certainly if one were able to choose such a way of life today it would be hard to find a more picturesque setting. St Herbert's friend and mentor was St Cuthbert, Bishop of Lindisfarne. According to Bede, both died at the same time on the same day, so great was their friendship.

Skiddaw from Applethwaite

Skiddaw, 1780

Both islands are well seen from the slopes of Skiddaw, Keswick's own mountain, which also had a famous hermit in the nineteenth century – a Scotsman named George Dodd. He was a harmless old soul for the most part, earning a few pence by painting portraits. He lived in a crudely furnished cave on the mountain but was well-read and could argue on most subjects, especially religion, as apparently he had been intended for the priesthood. His only failing was his liking for hard liquor: when he was drunk he became violent and often had to be horse-whipped out of the premises by angry landlords and then restrained in the police cells. Eventually he was forced to leave the area, being hounded by hooligans (who said brutish behaviour is a modern trait?) and gamekeepers. He died a pauper in his native land. Keep an eye open for his shadowy presence when you come down from the tops of Skiddaw late on a murky November day.

On occasions of state celebration or emergency, a great fire is lit by the citizens of Keswick on the top of Skiddaw. It could easily be seen from Carlisle in the days before bright street lighting. Robert Southey wrote a wonderful account of the scene at the bonfire that was lit there

73

to celebrate the victory of Waterloo on 21 August 1815. Amongst the distinguished company were the Wordsworth family, and it was the poet's misfortune to kick over the kettle that was being boiled to provide punch for refreshment. The consequence of this was that the party had to drink the rum that they had brought up with them undiluted and the journey down the mountain must have been hilarious; as some of them were too drunk to walk they were heaved on to the backs of horses and came down facing the tails of the beasts.

Chapter Six

# Legends, Lucks and Fairies

Hugh Hird, the Troutbeck Giant, was undoubtedly a man who was a legend in his time. Perhaps his feats grew with the telling, but there can be little doubt that such a man lived and was a hero in the district. It would be more difficult to prove that other giants of the neighbourhood had a place in history, though certainly enough of them have graves here. The best-known and most spectacular is the one in the churchyard at Penrith. Sir Walter Scott used to love to visit this monument, musing on the mystery of who lay buried beneath the great hog-backed stones. Even on his last journey into England, when

The Giant's Grave in the Church Yard, Penrith

75

the millions of words written in longhand by candlelight had taken their toll, he insisted on seeing the monument for the last time.

Present-day guidebooks speak of this being the grave of Owain Caesarius, King of Cumbria from 920 to 937. If the two great stones really mark the extremities of the person buried below, then he was indeed remarkable: they stand fifteen feet apart. Older guides borrowed more from the account written by Sullivan in 1857:

> Legend has it that he could not dwell in house or castle. The excavations in the banks of the Eamont, near its confluence with the Eden, well known as the Giant's Caves, were now appropriated as his residence, and he became a giant of doubtful character, 'a kind of knight-errant', who killed monster, man, and beast, and dragged them away to his den. But it is probable that we have here the engrafting of a hero tradition on that of a giant; for these caves are also said to have been the abode of one Isis, who seized men and cattle, and thereupon indiscriminately satisfied the cravings of his appetite.
>
> According to a tradition still extant, a fair lady from somewhere or other, where the fame of the giant had never reached, went down to walk on the riverbank, and unconscious of her danger, approached the cave of this dreadful being. She was seen by the lurking monster who suddenly issued from his den to seize her. Terror-stricken at the sight, the lady executed a most tremendous step across a wide cleft in the rocky bank, opening on the river beneath, and the giant in the act of pursuing her, missed his footing and broke his neck. Such was his end. The opening in the rock over which the lady so providentially passed, is called the Maiden's Step.

In 1670 the historian Sandford wrote that the grave at Penrith had been opened when he was a schoolboy. 'The great Long Shank bones and other bones of a man' had been found inside, but these were not so remarkable that measurements were given.

An early chronicler of Cumbria wrote of another impressive giant whose body was disinterred from its grave on the very edge of the district:

> In 1601 dug up near St Bees Head just before Christmas time a giant four yards and a half long, and was in complete armour; his teeth were six inches long and he was buried four yards deep in the ground now a cornfield. (Rev. Thomas Machel, 1698.)

Machel says that the giant's armour, with his great sword and battle-axe, were acquired by the Sandys family.

The Gosforth Cross

Gosforth is also in western Lakeland, to the south of St Bee's, on the boundary of the National Park. In its church and churchyard there are fascinating reminders of the pagan gods of the Vikings. The Gosforth Cross is a graceful, slender monument intricately carved more than a thousand years ago. Once there were four such crosses in this churchyard. While it bears some reminders of Christianity, the main themes of its carvings derive from the adventures of the pre-Christian gods, such as Thor. In a panel from another, broken, cross, Thor is shown in a boat with the giant Hymir fishing for the World Serpent (which was supposed to lie on the seabed, encircling the world with its tail in its mouth). Thor stole the head of Hymir's prize bull to use as bait for this expedition, but the giant probably never realised this, for when the serpent escaped from the god's line Thor was so annoyed that he 'raised his fist in a mad mortification and made a dead set at Hymir so that he up-ended him into the sea and the last Thor saw of him was the soles of his feet. Then Thor waded ashore.' (Quoted from *The Lost Gods of England* by Brian Branston.)

Mallerstang Edge forms part of the border between Cumbria and Yorkshire, overlooking the upper valley of the River Eden. Over this remote country ruled a king named Uther Pendragon, a cruel and despotic giant who seems an unlikely father for King Arthur, yet often wickedness spawns goodness, as it appears to have done in this case. He is supposed to have used sorcery to seduce Igraine, Duchess of Cornwall. The result of this shameful union was Arthur, the chivalrous knight *par excellence*.

When he was not terrorising the neighbourhood, Uther spent much of his time attempting to divert the waters of the Eden so that his castle, Pendragon, might have a moat. He was always unsuccessful in this, as is shown by the ancient rhyme

> *Let Uther Pendragon do what he can*
> *Eden shall run as Eden ran.*

Uther died besieged in his castle when his enemies, failing to dislodge him by force of arms, poisoned the water supply. The scant ruins that the intrepid explorer to these remote parts will find today are the remains of the castle built by Sir Hugh de Morville in the twelfth century. He was one of the murderers of St Thomas à Becket, but after this despicable act was unable to live at Pendragon as he was for ever seeing the face of the dying archbishop etched in the

Thor in the boat with the giant Hymir

Pendragon Castle

crags of Wild Boar Fell. Not surprisingly the castle and its surroundings are haunted by all manner of ghosts and demons, including the enormous figure of Uther Pendragon himself.

It has been suggested that the name Uther Pendragon was adopted by a later owner of the castle, Robert de Clifford. He had two motives for doing this: he lived during the time when the chivalrous ideals exemplified by the Court of King Arthur were being resurrected. Thus Mallerstang Castle was renamed 'Pendragon' sometime after 1309 and Clifford took Uther's name as a *nom de guerre* in the Arthurian tourneys that became fashionable in the time of Edward I. Secondly, Clifford had relatives and ancestors from the Royal Family of Wales and an estate on the borders of that country. Thus he would have known Arthurian legend well (perhaps believing that he was a descendant of Arthur himself) and so delighted in promoting it in his province.

Medieval tournaments were often staged in the amphitheatre adapted from a prehistoric earthwork at Eamont Bridge, Penrith, which is close to another Clifford property, Brougham Castle. This

80

A 'gentle knight' of the tourneys

has been known as Arthur's Round Table since the early sixteenth century, and obviously it would have made an excellent site for medieval tournaments with all their feasting and jousting. Sir Walter Scott made it the scene of a colourful pageant in *The Bridal of Triermain.*

Other places with strong connections with King Arthur in Cumbria include Carlisle, once his capital, where he is supposed to have held court, and Ravenglass, thought by some to be Avalon.Here Arthur would rest until his wounds healed, and then re-emerge to restore the fortunes of the British peoples. Experts can argue forever about these locations, but we will never know for sure. These legends were born more than sixteen hundred years ago, and it seems that they survived the Dark Ages only on the lips of minstrels and storytellers. However one legend of King Arthur and his Knights has a rare Lakeland flavour to it: it is called *The Marriage of Sir Gawaine,* and a copy of the romance, written in verse, survives from the fifteenth century. Tarn Wadling, which was drained in the last century, was situated near the church at High Hesket, midway between Penrith and Carlisle.

The romance begins with the King riding by the Tarn and being accosted by a fierce giant, at least twice the height of a normal man, who challenged him, saying that he could either fight or pay a ransom. If he chooses the latter, then he must return on New Year's Day with the answer to the giant's riddle: 'What thing it is that a woman will most desire?'

King Arthur collected hundreds of answers to this, and was on his way back to the tarn with them when he met a hideously ugly woman:

> *And as he rode over a more,*
> *Hee see a lady where shee sate*
> *Betwixt an oke and a greene hollen;*
> *She was cladd in red scarlett.*
>
> *Then thereas shold have stood her mouth,*
> *Then there was sett her eye;*
> *The other was in her forhead fast,*
> *The way that she might see.*
>
> *Her nose was crooked and turn'd outward,*
> *Her mouth stood foul a-wry;*
> *A worse form'd lady than shee was,*
> *Never man saw with his eye.*

The woman accused the King of behaving discourteously to her because of her ugliness, but said that she understood the reason for this since she alone knew the correct answer to the riddle that he had been given. Arthur, desperately seizing any opportunity, begged to be given the solution, promising her the hand of Gawain, his cousin, should it defeat the giant.

Sure enough the giant was standing menacingly by the Tarn, and demanded the answer to the riddle, otherwise he would slay the King and take his lands.

*And then bespoke him noble Arthur*
*And bad him hold his hand:*
*'And give me leave to speak my mind*
*In defence of all my land.'*

*He said, 'As I came over a more,*
*I see a lady where shee sate*
*Between an oke and a green hollen;*
*Shee was clad in red scarlett.*

*And she says a woman will have her will,*
*And this is all her cheef desire:*
*Doe me right, as thou art a baron of sckill,*
*This is thy ransom and all thy hyer'.*

The giant was angry at this, informing Arthur that it was his sister who had given him the answer to the riddle. And so the King returned to his Knights to tell them of his promise to the ugly woman.

When King Arthur explained that he had betrothed one of them to a monstrous woman, in order to save his life, only Sir Gawaine did not flinch from the prospect of such a marriage. His bride was duly found in the Forest of Inglewood, and after the marriage-feast she was brought to bed by her husband. As he embraced her, she changed into a woman of startling beauty, and told him that he had the choice of her being ugly by day and beautiful at night, or *vice versa*. In reply he tenderly said that this decision could only be taken by her.

This reply broke a spell woven on her in her youth by a jealous stepmother. At last she was given the thing that a woman most desires, her will, and resumed her proper, beautiful. form both by day and by night.

Many of the great Cumbrian families believed that their fortunes depended on the careful protection of ancient talismans that had come to them in strange circumstances. These 'Lucks' were carefully preserved, though in one instance the Luck survives while the family has failed. This is the Luck of Edenhall, now in the Victoria and Albert Museum.

The Edenhall Luck is the oldest of the Lucks of Lakeland (at least six families had them), dating from the thirteenth century. It is an enamelled glass vase probably brought back from Syria after one of the Crusades. Its case of boiled leather also survives and bears the letters IHS, the initials of Jesus Christ Saviour, in Greek (which suggests that it may have originally been a chalice).

Edenhall is a village close to Penrith, but the house, the home of the Musgrave family, was demolished in 1934. The legend about the Luck says that it was found by one of the servants when he went to fetch water from St Cuthbert's Well, not far from the house. A crowd of fairies were dancing around the glass and when he picked it up they disappeared, singing:

*If e'er that glass should break or fall*
*Farewell the luck of Edenhall*

The Musgraves carefully preserved the Luck for many centuries, though it must have come close to destruction on occasions when the Duke of Wharton visited one of the early baronets. The Duke 'was accustomed, after his revels and amongst his boon companions, to toss up the cup in the air – when he, or some one in attendance, caught it again!' The last baronet left England to live in India in the 1930s, leaving the precious glass in the care of the Victoria and Albert Museum.

Digressing slightly, it appears that Eden Hall itself had a ghost. The following appeared in *Cumbria* in October, 1972:

My grandmother, Ellen Whiteside (née Bentley) was employed when she was a young girl by the Musgraves of Eden Hall. She told us that shortly before she was married she went to visit the housekeeper and stayed the night.

She slept with the housekeeper's niece in a room that had been the night nursery. During the night they were wakened by someone coming into the room. They heard the window blind being adjusted, drawers being opened and closed, and the fire poked, even though it was summer and there was no fire. The invisible intruder's footsteps then approached their bed and paused, before they left the room.

In the morning they told the housekeeper of their experience and she scoffed, yet soon afterwards my grandmother learned of a nurserymaid who had worked at the Hall. On her deathbed the maid recounted a lovely dream about Eden Hall. She had been back to the Hall, visited the night nursery, and remembered carrying out the routines practised by the ghost. On investigation it transpired that the dream was experienced on the same night that my grandmother had spent at the Hall.

The Luck of Muncaster Castle is another piece of ancient glassware. This still resides in the house that it was given to, though in this case the benefactor was a King, and not the Little People.

After the Battle of Hexham in 1463, the defeated Lancastrian King, Henry VI, was left a fugitive, wandering over the fells and seeking shelter where he could. Having been refused hospitality at Irton Hall he was discovered by shepherds and brought to Muncaster Castle

The Luck of Muncaster

where Sir John Pennington was pleased to entertain him. There is a tablet in Muncaster Church which is inscribed:

Holie Kinge Harrye gave Sir John a brauce wrkyd glass cuppe ... whylles the familie shold keep hit unbrecken they shold gretely thryve.

A 'pepperpot' monument near the castle marks the spot where the shepherds are supposed to have found the wandering king, and his portrait holding the Luck may be seen there.

The Luck of Workington was also given by royalty, being the gift of Mary, Queen of Scots to Sir Henry Curwen. She enjoyed his hospitality at Workington Hall on 16 May 1568, the first night of her exile in England (all subsequent nights in this country were spent as a prisoner). This Luck is a beautiful goblet made of agate and may be seen at Belle Isle, Windermere. Many people regarded the fate of Mary as a martyrdom, as they did the death of King Henry VI, 'Holie King Harry', and since these monarchs were held to rule by divine right the Lucks of Muncaster and Workington were regarded almost as holy relics. They had properties that the Lucks given by elves or fairies could never achieve.

Burrell Green is a farm near Great Salkeld which has another of the Lucks of Lakeland. This is a brass dish, just over sixteen inches in diameter, with its centre decorated with a twisted rose. Around this the words 'Mary, Mother of Jesus, Saviour of Men' could once be deciphered. More recent lettering decorated the outside of the vessel:

> *If e'er this dish be sold or gi'en,*
> *Farewell the Luck of Burrell Green.*

Marjorie Rowling, in *The Folklore of the Lake District*, says the date of the dish is about 1417 when it was given to a daughter of the house on the occasion of her marriage to a 'King' of Mardale. Again a servant, sent to the well, encountered Little People (hob-goblins in this instance) who said that if they were given food they would bless the wedding. When this was brought to them they gave the servant the dish. There is a tradition that the dish falls from its place when the property changes hands.

Martindale lies above the southern shore of Ullswater, a lonely place even in this age of mechanised transport. Appropriately it was here in the 1850s that fairies were seen in the Lake District for the last time.

Ullswater

The event was witnessed by a man named Jack Wilson who was returning to his home one evening over Sandwick Rigg.

He suddenly perceived before him, in the glimpses of the moon, a large company of fairies intensely engaged in their favourite diversions. He drew near unobserved, and presently descried a stee (ladder) reaching from amongst them up into a cloud. But no sooner was the presence of mortal discovered than all made a hasty retreat up the stee. Jack rushed forward, doubtless firmly determined to follow them into fairy-land, but arrived too late. They had effected their retreat, and quickly drawing up the stee, they shut the cloud, and disappeared. And in the concluding words of Jack's story, which afterwards became proverbial in that neighbourhood, 'yance gane, ae gane, and niver saw mair o' them'.
(Jeremiah Sullivan, *Cumberland and Westmorland Ancient and Modern*, 1857.)

Of course anyone witnessing such an event today would immediately report a sighting of a UFO.

Elves and Fairies, Sullivan, continues, are fallen angels − less harmful to humans than they might be since they themselves were once seduced. They are always present at events such as fairs, funerals or weddings, though they are seldom seen. They help themselves to the greatest delicacies on display at such feasts, leaving 'shadowy forms' in their place. This might explain the food at the M6 service areas!

Fairies were able to tell miners in which direction to dig for rich lodes of copper. They often guarded the hoards of treasure said to be hidden beneath mounds all over the Lake District, and woe betide anyone who tried to take it. A story from Lanercost Priory tells of a man returning home at night who was dragged from his horse by a crowd of fairies and would have been taken through the doorway of their magic hill had he not been carrying a page from a Bible in his pocket. Iron or steel also worked as charms against the powers of fairies, as did crosses or rosaries.

A swarth was (or is?) a supernatural being akin to the fairies. It performed the same function in the North of England as a banshee does in Ireland – foretelling death.

There is a person now living in the county who fully believes the swarth, or likeness of his nephew appeared to him the night he was lost at sea. He was aroused from sleep by a noise, as of some one clinging to the window of his bedroom. He looked round and distinctly saw the face and form of his nephew, then on his journey to India. After gazing into the room a short while, the apparition seemed to fall to the ground with a dull, heavy sound. The uncle rose from bed, and looked out of the window, but nothing could be seen. It is thought that if the swarth is seen late in the day, and on the road towards church, the person to whom it is like will soon die; if it is seen in the early part of the morning, and going in any other direction, it betokens health and long life.
(J.Sullivan.)

Another way of learning who was to die in the parish over the next year was to keep vigil in the churchyard on St Mark's Eve (April 24). Those who waited there during the hours before and after midnight would see the spirits of friends and neighbours who would die during the year pass through the porch of the church.

It was also possible to make forecasts of marriages, the hour of midnight on Hallow'een being particularly propitious. Unfortunately the following example is also rather morbid.

A young girl in the Hesket district of Caldbeck was sent by her mistress into the barn of the farm, which had doors on both the east and west sides. It was midnight, and the unsuspecting girl was asked if she had seen anyone there. 'No-one but the master,' the girl replied, 'he came in at one door and went out of the other.'

'Be good to my children then,' said her mistress, who died within the year. Sure enough the farmer married the girl, who always remembered the words of her husband's first wife and took good care of the children.

The superstitions and customs associated with death often throw light on the spirit world. In the west of Cumbria it was believed that the Death Light, a glowing blue light, showed the passage of the spirit out of the body at death. It would follow the path that the cortège would take at the funeral.

All the mirrors in the house were covered while a dead person was lying in a house, for it was considered to be extremely unlucky should the spirit catch sight of a reflected image of itself. People visiting the house for the lying-in used to touch the body. This served two

purposes: if the corpse had been murdered and it was touched by the guilty party, then it would begin to bleed; also if the hand laid on the body felt cold to one's own flesh it meant that that person would die within the year.

The custom of visiting the beehives to tell the bees of their owner's death is found all over England, and was certainly practised in Cumbria. Crumbs from the funeral feast were left out for them, and the hives decorated with black ribbons. It was believed that unless these courtesies were observed the bees would leave the hives.

Another belief, rather less kind to all concerned, was that a dying person could not pass away if he were lying on a bed containing pigeon feathers. Thus a lingering invalid might be taken off his soft mattress and left on the bare floor to expire, a course of action which must have invariably speeded the process and confirmed the truth of the superstition.

Chapter Seven

# Penrith and the East

Kirkby Stephen lies on the very edge of Cumbria, in its south-eastern corner. One of its traditions has it that the Last Boar of Cumbria was hunted down on Wild Boar Fell by Sir Richard Musgrave of Hartley Castle, early in the fifteenth century. When his grave was opened up in the nineteenth century a boar's tusk was found resting on his breast, lending weight to the legend. Just to the south of the town is Stenkrith Bridge where there is a deep crack in the bedrock. A strange roaring sound is to be heard from this cleft, supposed to be made by the Devil's Mustard Mill, where damned souls are kept working by Old Nick to make a condiment hot enough to suit his taste.

Over the centuries Cumbria has suffered more than its fair share of despotic aristocracy, most of whom return to haunt the places that they tyrannised. Kirkby Stephen had the Whartons, who in fairness also had generous and kind heads of the family to counterbalance the cruel despots. The swashbuckling Sir Thomas Wharton, Warden of the Marches and Scourge of the Scots, had the ten-foot-high walls which surround the deer-park built in 1560 by workmen dragooned into the task for wages of one penny a day or a peck of barley meal'. Later, the dissolute Duke of Wharton of Jacobean times was a famous member of the Hellfire Club.

But it is an ancestor of his who haunts the locality. This is the 'Wicked Lord Wharton' who brought so much cruelty and suffering to the district in Tudor times. As lord of the manor of Ravenstonedale he was able to preside over his own aptly-named Peculiar Court, which was empowered to deliver the death sentence. The gallows stood on the hilltop behind Wharton Hall and woe betide anyone who defied his wishes. He was the archetypal 'wicked squire' and was ruthless to tenants and gentry alike. It would seem that no-one was sorry to hear of his death which came after a sudden stroke afflicted him as he rode alone over Ash Fell. He was left blind but managed to stagger back to the Hall where he later died. His ghost haunts the nightmare path he

The Slaying of the Last Wild Boar

took home, outstretched hands groping for the long wall which surrounds the park.

Orton, due west of Kirkby Stephen and close to the motorway, was famous, or notorious, for its boggle in the early nineteenth century. This misty creature, a glowing yet shapeless outline, would seem to lie in wait for late wayfarers. What makes this boggle remarkable is the way it resisted exorcism. This account of the event is from *Cumberland and Westmorland Ancient and Modern*, written by Jeremiah Sullivan in 1857:

> It was said that a 'Methodee man' (Methodist preacher) was brought to exorcise the boggle, thus assuming for 'Methodee men' the power supposed at one time to belong exclusively to Catholic priests. But the exorcist on receiving a blow with his own hat on the back of his head, very properly declined any further interference. On the whole, as far as local history is concerned, there is every appearance that the last page of the chapter of boggles is turned for ever.

Orton

Mardale Green

For the sake of future ghosthunters, let us hope that this is not the case.

Before the building of the motorway, the A6 was one of the busiest roads in Britain, and one of the most dangerous. Its passage over Shap Fell was especially hazardous in winter and it was the firm belief of locals that the sight of a black dog presaged a fatal accident. The animal always appeared at the same spot, running in front of cars for a short distance before leaping over a stone parapet below which was a drop of three hundred feet. The black dog made newspaper headlines in the autumn of 1937 when it was seen on several nights.

To the west of Shap lies the Haweswater Reservoir which covers one of the most beautiful and secluded of Lakeland valleys – Mardale. This vanished in the winter of 1936–7 when it was flooded to hold water for the city of Manchester. Mardale village lacked a church until 1729 and people who died there had to be strapped on the backs of horses and taken up the Corpse Road over Mardale Common and Swindale to be buried at Shap. There is a legend (used by Hall Caine in his novel *Shadow of a Crime*) that one native of Mardale once died with an undiscovered crime on his conscience. His body was carried up the Corpse Road in the usual way, slung across the back of a horse, but a frightful storm broke and a clap of thunder made the horse bolt. The horse, and its grisly burden, were not seen for three months, when, in fact, the dead man's crime was revealed.

Above Haweswater is High Street, a mountain with a fine plateau famous for its gatherings of shepherds in the old days. They used to come from all over the district to identify stray sheep and also partake in traditional fell sports – wrestling, horse racing, running and drinking; particularly the latter, and at over 2,700 feet above sea level! The ascent of High Street from the head of Haweswater is a favourite of Wainwright, and takes the fellwalker past Blea Water Crag. In the 1970s Wainwright saw a pair of golden eagles here, but our interest is in a remarkable fall suffered by a man named Dixon in 1762. He was fox-hunting, and attempting to climb this crag he missed his foothold and fell several hundreds of feet, bouncing three times off outcrops on the way. Although terribly bruised when he landed he was not badly hurt and was able to shout to his companions the way that the fox had

Small Water Tarn, looking into Mardale

gone. Subsequently the crag was known locally as 'Dixon's Three Jumps'. Sadly a schoolboy was not so fortunate in a recent fall from Bleawater Crag, and was killed.

The Lyvennet Valley is famous for its tales of treasure. At Crosby Ravensworth the Hall was a favourite residence of the Threlkeld family, understandably, as the house stood close to the old church in a charming valley with the river sparkling nearby. They kept all their valuables in the undercroft of the massive pele tower, guarded by 'a gurt white bull' which roamed the pasture just outside. It is said that this creature still guards the tower, even though this was demolished some centuries ago. Another version comes from Sullivan:

> It is recorded in a manuscript history of Crosby Ravensworth, that a Dobbie at Crosby Hall revealed to a farmer the place in which he would find a treasure. 'It would not, perhaps, be considered a faithful history', says the writer, 'were no mention made of a certain extraordinary being, which is said to have paid nightly visits to the Hall about this time, to the no small terror and astonishment of the family then belonging to it; which, whether a real preternatural apparition, or whether the effect of some clandestine knavery, or whether a phantom of the imagination only, did certainly at that time excite more public curiosity, furnish more subject for marvellous anecdote, and will, I believe, be longer remembered than any living lord that owned the place before or after.' At what date it commenced its gloomy walks we cannot learn, all the old records being silent upon the subject; but tradition says, it left the place after the demolition of the old tower, and on taking leave gave an old gentleman, the farmer at the Hall, information of some hidden treasure, and also a very friendly intimation of the exact time and manner of his death, which old people say, with much confidence, and within their remembrance, did happen accordingly.

It may be, of course, that the dobbie sometimes took the form of a white bull.

Further downstream, at Morland, there is a strange earthwork called Skelly Warke where a great treasure was said to lie hidden. This was mysteriously guarded by 'a dark gipsy-looking lad' until in 1827 archaeologists arrived to excavate the mound. Then the gipsy lad disappeared, literally, into thin air, never to be seen again. The antiquarians found eleven skeletons buried below the mound, each wearing a golden armlet.

Elliott O'Donnell wrote about ghosts for more than fifty years. He

The Druids' Circle

was a prolific writer whose work was enjoyed by a wide readership. If he had a fault it was in being vague about locations. In *Haunted Britain* he prints a letter from a correspondent about a 'Druidical Circle in Westmorland' which I believe is most likely to be one of those to be found near Crosby Ravensworth – Oddendale, perhaps; Hardendale; or Iron Hill near Harberwain. His correspondent wrote:

The only personal experience which I have had happened at a Druid's Circle. The phenomena consisted of a sickly, death-like smell, and the sense of some 'presence' approaching. I hastily retreated to a distance and saw a figure, clad in white or light grey, glide from the adjoining wood and vanish near the largest stone of the circle. I may say that the circle is half in a pine wood, and that a stone wall has been built across the circle, cutting it into two parts. The cause of the phenomena probably is that the largest stone was dug up in the late seventies of the last century. An urn was found, and is now in a museum. I have been told, on reliable testimony, that manifestations of an unpleasant nature followed the lifting of a stone in the celebrated circle of 'Long Meg and her daughters', near Penrith in Cumberland.

Reagill lies above the Lyvennet Valley, a mile or so to the north of Crosby Ravensworth. Reagill Grange was once very troubled by ghosts, one of the most haunted houses in Westmorland. Jessica Lofthouse, in *North Country Folklore*, tells of finding a dobbie stone here (a holed stone, giving protection against evil spirits). It was lying on the floor, the rusty nail from which it had been hung from a beam having corroded away some time before. She writes that the Grange

> ... must have trusted in its dobbie stone to bring good luck or keep evil away. Among its many hauntings was the apparition of a lady in white, and one which opened and shut gates, and a ghost hound of enormous size. The white lady took shape when a Major White of Reagill rode home at midnight. The white thing in a tree was an owlet, thought he, and fired his gun, whereupon it grew bigger and bigger and leapt to ride postillion behind him, hanging on like grim death. When he reached the hall he was dragged indoors battered and bleeding, his horse wet with sweat and staring madly as all mounts do when hag-ridden.

Another story from this district, again told by Miss Lofthouse, concerned two labourers who, returning from an evening's heavy drinking, saw some sheep in an area of woodland where they did not belong. But on attempting to drive the animals out they found that two strange forms were working from the opposite direction, pushing the animals back into the wood. This toing and froing went on for some time until a flash of moonlight revealed that one of the mysterious drovers had horns, whereupon both men fled home, doubtless swearing never to touch the hard stuff again, not till next payday anyway!

A further legend of this neighbourhood concerns Bewley Castle, not far from Appleby. In the sixteenth century this was the home of Sir Richard Musgrave, who one evening left with his family to visit friends in a nearby village. An old housekeeper was left in charge and she busied herself by making rush lights, dipping the plaited rush wicks into liquid tallow. As she did this a knock sounded at the door, and opening it she found a tall, weather-beaten woman standing outside, who begged for food and drink in a harsh, croaky voice. As was the custom, she was offered hospitality – bread and home-brew – and then, feeling the effect of the beer and the roaring fire, she

Bewley Castle

dropped off to sleep. At this point the housekeeper noticed that this was no woman that she had let in: her unladylike posture revealed that she was wearing riding-boots and spurs. Realising that she and the castle were in danger from such an impostor, the housekeeper picked up the ladle and poured boiling tallow into the gaping mouth of the sleeping figure. It must have been a terrible way to be awoken from a doze! As he lay writhing in agony the brave woman rang the alarm bell to bring the family home. Sir Richard and his son arrived just in time to find the remainder of the robber-band fleeing. The intruder was revealed as Belted Will Scott, a notable outlaw, whose body was dragged far from the house and buried beneath some trees. As the story in dialect concludes: '. . . though unshrouded or shriven he got extreme unction. At least summat like it, wi' het cannel grease.'

It is only fair to add that more or less the same story is told about several other locations, the most authentic coming from the old Spittal Inn, high on Bowes Moor (you pass it on the A66). In this version, told by William Henderson in 1866, the date is given as 1795, and particular mention is made of the woman lighting the infamous Hand

Appleby

of Glory to ensure that the household remained asleep. The Hand of Glory was the hand of a dead man which clutched a candle made from revolting ingredients, including the fat of a suckling child and the flesh of a hanged man. It could only be extinguished by dowsing it with fresh milk, which is just what the quick-witted maid at the Old Spittal managed to do.

For much of the year Appleby is a quiet market town of about two and a half thousand souls situated between the foothills of the Lakes and the Pennines. For a week or so in June, though, the place comes alive as gipsies from all over the country congregate here for the horse-fair which is the largest in Britain. Caravans, stalls, tethered horses and other livestock all crowd along the verge of the lane that leads to Long Marton. This has been the site of the fair for generations, and the gipsy dealers have resisted all proposals to move to a more practicable location. One suggestion was that the fair should be held on nearby Hanging Shaw, an open expanse of moor offering much more space. This was immediately rejected by the travelling people who knew of the gruesome reputation of the place. As its name suggests, this was where the town's malefactors suffered the ultimate punishment, their bodies being left swinging to serve as a warning to others (its alternative name is Gallows Hill). Not surprisingly the place is well haunted by a variety of restless spirits.

Appleby's most famous ghost appears to date from the Cromwellian era. She was somewhat affectionately known as Peg Sneddle, though her correct name appears to have been Elizabeth Sleddall, who was married to Lancelot Machell of Crackenthorpe Hall. The reason for the use of her maiden name by the ghost is unknown, but it seems that she was upset by the terms of her husband's will and would appear like a banshee whenever a head of the Machell family was about to die. An old account says that the countryfolk of the district believed that Peg Sneddle was a disreputable lady when alive and became even more troublesome after death. They waited for a time when the River Eden was flowing low and then, taking her body from its grave in the churchyard, reburied her in the river-bed beneath a massive boulder of Shap granite. A Catholic priest was called upon to read the service of exorcism, committing her to remain there for 999 years. Nevertheless she still walks once a year, in September, when she rises from the river to enter the Hall through a blocked-up window.

Whether this lady is the same as the one who dashes around the locality in a carriage driven by six black horses is open to doubt. This, it seems to me, would more likely be Elizabeth Sleddall, who could not even bear to own to her husband's name after his death. An account of the village includes the tale that the old keeper of the tollgate used to tell:

. . . of old Mistress Machell driving through the gate in offended style when the Helm Wind was raging. She was seated in a large old-fashioned carriage drawn by six coal-black horses with long tails, with flaming eyes and nostrils. The coachman wore a three-cornered lace hat and had huge black boots. Other attendants followed on horses. Suddenly with a wild blast the turnpike gate was burst open, and with long unhallowed shrieks, the wan face of Mistress Machell in the carriage disappeared into the midnight darkness.

When the Helm Wind is blowing and storms raging on the fell, 'Peg' is said to be in her tantrums, and in more gracious mood in fine weather. An old oak tree that formerly existed in the neighbourhood of Crackenthorpe was called Sleddall's Oak. A female figure, supposed to be that of Mistress

Machell's ghost, was seen thereunder when any misfortune was about to befall any member of the Machell family.
(*History of Crackenthorpe* by Lionel Cresswell, 1933.)

Sadly, the direct line of Machells came to an end with the death of the heir in the First World War, so presumably Crackenthorpe Hall is now free of ghostly visitations.

The Helm Wind mentioned above is an icy blast that is usually said to blow from Fiends Fell, to the north. Its seemingly unnatural chill, its fierceness, and the suddeness of its coming gave it a supernatural reputation. Hutchinson's *History of Cumberland*, 1794 – 7, carries an excellent description of this meteorological phenomenon:

Upon the summits of this lofty ridge of mountains, there frequently hangs a vast volume of clouds, in a sullen and drowsy state, having little movement; this heavy collection of vapours often extends several miles in length, and dips itself from the summit, half way down to the base of those eminences; and frequently, at the same time, the other mountains in view are clear of mist, and shew no signs of rain. This *helm*, or cloud, exhibits an awful and solemn appearance, tinged with white from the sun's rays that strike the upper parts, and spreads a gloom below, over the inferior parts of the mountains, like the shadows of night. When this collection of vapour first begins to gather upon the hills, there is to be observed hanging about it, a black strip of cloud, continually flying off, and fed from the white part, which is the real *helm*; this strip is called the *helm-bar*, as, during its appearance, the winds are thought to be resisted by it; for, on its dispersal, they rage vehemently on the vallies beneath. The direction of the *helm-bar* is parallel to that part of the main cloud or collection of vapour, that is tinged with white by being struck with the sun's rays; the *bar* appears in continual agitation, as boiling, or struggling with contrary blasts; while the *helm* all this time keeps a motionless station. When the *bar* is dispersed, the winds that issue from the *helm* are sometimes extremely violent; but that force seems in proportion to the real current of winds which blow at a distance from the mountains, and which are frequently in a contrary direction, and then the *helm-wind* does not extend above two or three miles; without these impediments it seldom sweeps over a larger track than twelve miles, perhaps from the mere resistance of the lower atmosphere. It is remarkable, that at the base of the mountain the blasts are much less violent than in the middle region; and yet the hurricane is sometimes impetuous even there, bearing everything before it, when at the distance of a few miles there is a dead calm, and a sunny sky. The spring is most favourable to this phenomenon, the *helm-wind* will sometimes blow for a fortnight, till the air in the lower regions, warmed before by the influence of the sun, is thereby rendered piercing cold.

Gerald Findler (*Lakeland Ghosts*) speaks of Brackenby Moor being haunted (also known as Brackenber, this is in the area of the Golf Course). A murder once took place nearby, and subsequently people saw 'ghosts, flames, and other manifestations near where the murderer used to live'.

A final tale of Appleby belongs to the end of the eighteenth century when a troublesome ghost known as Old Shepherd had to be laid. A Catholic priest condemned him to lie outside the house which he had disturbed, beneath a large stone. Not long afterwards celebrations were held in honour of an election triumph and a large 'bone-fire' was lit close to the house. Whilst the party was in full swing it was noticed that the shade of Old Shepherd emerged from beneath his stone 'in the shape of a large white something; but he turned off sideways, and *sailed* down the "beck", in which they could hear him splashing like a horse.' Not too unnerved by the boggle's behaviour, the party put out their fire and moved downstream to a place where firewood was lying; but the ghost soon followed and after this the festivities were abandoned.

In a magical twinkling of an eye we now fly to the other side of the motorway, to the district between Hackthorpe and the lower end of Ullswater, which is particularly rich in ghosts and legends. At Hackthorpe itself a farmer who lived at the Hall was led to treasure by an apparition which took the form of a calf. He noticed that this unlikely-seeming ghost always vanished by a stone cattle-trough. When the trough was lifted he found a great hoard of gold hidden underneath, enough for him to buy two estates in Cumberland. It's a pity that the Inland Revenue don't fall for such stories today!

However the epicentre of the district's ghostly activities must be Lowther Hall (the Hall has long been demolished and its successor, Lowther Castle, is just a spectacular shell: a wildlife park occupies its grounds). The cause of the celebrated disturbances here was Sir James Lowther, created the first Earl Lonsdale in 1784. He was a violent man, who loved field sports as much as he hated paying his debts. His debt to Wordsworth's father, amounting to five thousand pounds, became subject to a court case which after several years found in

103

Goldrill Beck and Ullswater

favour of the Wordsworths: but Lord Lonsdale ignored the judgement and refused to pay, the money still being owed at his death in 1802. It was not as though he was at all short of cash – he earned a fortune when the Industrial Revolution transformed his lands in West Cumberland – rich seams of coal lay beneath them. Of course it might be argued that had he paid the money, Wordsworth would have lacked the poverty essential to a good poet. In 1857 Jeremiah Sullivan braved the displeasure of the Lonsdales, the most powerful family in Cumbria, by writing:

> Westmorland never produced a more famous boggle – infamous as a man, famous as a boggle – than Jemmy Lowther, well known, for want of a more appropriate name, as the 'bad Lord Lonsdale'. This notorious character, who seemed the transmigration of the worst and coarsest feudal baron ever imported into England by the Conqueror, became a still greater terror to the country after death, than he had been during his life. He was with difficulty buried; and whilst the clergyman was praying over him, he very nearly knocked the reverend gentleman from his desk. When placed in

Lowther Castle

the grave, the power of creating alarm was not interred with his bones. There were disturbances in the Hall, noises in the stables; neither men nor animals were suffered to rest. Jemmy's 'coach and six' is still remembered and spoken of, from which we are probably to understand that he produced a noise, as boggles frequently do, like the equipage of this description. There is nothing said of his shape, or whether he appeared at all; but it is certain he made himself audible. The Hall became almost uninhabitable, and out of doors there was constant danger of meeting the miscreant ghost. In desperate cases of this kind, it appears, there is no assistance to be had, except from a Catholic priest, one reason being that the exorcism must be made in Latin. Jemmy, however – obstinate old boggle! – stood a long siege; and when at length he offered terms of capitulation, was only willing to go to the Red Sea for a year and a day. But it was decided that these terms should not be accepted; the priest read on until he fully overpowered the tyrant, and *laid* him under a large rock called Wallow Crag, and laid him for ever.

In fact there is some debate as to just where the unruly spirit rests.

Some say that Jemmy's body was disinterred and reburied on Hugh Laithe's Pike in the hope that his spirit would feel more at home with such a grand view. Wallow Crag is close by, also overlooking Haweswater.

Penrith is more famous for its giant than its ghost, though a skeletal phantom has been seen from time to time on Beacon Hill, usually identified as being the ghost of Thomas Nicholson who was executed for murder on 31 August 1767. His body, enclosed in an iron cage, hung from a gibbet here for many years, though it was gone when the young Wordsworth passed by:

> *I led my horse, and, stumbling on, at length*
> *Came to a bottom, where in former times*
> *A murderer had been hung in iron chains.*
> *The gibbet-mast had mouldered down, the bones*
> *And iron cage were gone; but on the turf,*
> *Hard by, soon after that fell deed was wrought,*
> *Some unknown hand had carved the murderer's name.*

The stone circle of Mayborough, just to the south of the town, rivals Long Meg but is not so famous. Magic is supposed to protect the circle: once men were sent with gunpowder to break up the stones. They quickly gave up their attempts when a remarkable storm broke over their heads without any warning.

Nobody can fail to be intrigued by the romantic ruins of Brougham Castle that stand boldly by the river in full view of the main road to Scotch Corner. It was a stronghold of the Cliffords, and its most famous tradition was recorded in the Memoirs of Lady Anne Clifford (who restored Brougham as well as several other Clifford castles). She wrote in 1658:

> This summer, by some few mischievous people secretly in the night, there was broken off and taken down from that tree, neare the paile of Whinfield Park (which for that cause was called the Hart's Horne Tree) one of those old Hart's Horns which (as is mentioned in the summerie of my Ancestors, Robert Lord Clifford's Life) was sett upp in the year 1333 att a general huntinge, when Edward Ballioll, then King of Scots . . . lay for a while in the said Lord Clifford's castle in Westmorland, where the King hunted a greate stag which was killed neare the said Oak Tree. In memory whereof the hornes were nayled up in it, growing as it were naturally in the Tree. . . .

Brougham Castle

The death of the 'greate stag' and Hercules

The 'greate stag' was apparently put up by a hound, Hercules, on Whinfell, and the chase led to Redkirks in Scotland and back again. On its return to the park the stag leapt the fence but the effort was too great and it died where it landed. Hercules failed to jump the fence and died close by, also succumbing to exhaustion.

There is said to be another bricked-up skull in Brougham Hall. Like others in the region it could not tolerate being taken from the house and always returned, a grisly reminder of mortality. It was also held to be responsible for a series of accidents and disturbances that beset the house in its absence. Finally it was bricked up in a secret location where, presumably, it rests happy.

Stainton is a village on the western side of Penrith. Once a church or abbey stood on its outskirts and human bones were dug up from amongst the ruined stonework. Sullivan tells of a sombre legend that concerned this place:

> In the course of 'reformation' the lands belonging to this religious edifice fell into the hands of a certain baron, a man of reckless violence, who lived somewhere thereabouts. He had a number of men employed in the removal of the church, or what ruins remained thereof, probably with the intention of building a house fit to lodge a man of increased wealth: and one day, in consequence of some scruples of the labourers, or some hesitation in the execution of his commands, he came himself to the grounds. His orders were very positive, and accompanied with various threats, and doubtless some profane language. Having delivered himself of these, he rode off in the direction of Penruddock, and had gained the summit of the rising ground, looking backwards as he went, when his horse fell under him, and he broke his neck. On the very spot from which the fool looked back in triumph, his soul was required of him. The place is called Baron's Hill: it is about half a mile out of Stainton.

And so, of course, the ghostly figure of a man on horseback has occasionally been seen here.

Dacre Castle is to the west of Stainton, guarding the lower reach of Ullswater. The Dacres were once one of the most powerful families in the region, but in the end, through lack of a male heir, their fortunes were merged with those of the Howards, Dukes of Norfolk. The last of the line was Thomas Dacre who thought the succession was secure when a male heir was born to him after three daughters. However like many another before him, Thomas often succumbed to the charms of

Dacre Castle

local maidens. Unfortunately he brought to grief the daughter of one of his tenant farmers, who believed him when he told her that he loved her, and bore him a bastard son. When he disowned this child the girl took herself off and was later found drowned in the stream nearby. The grief-stricken mother then called down a curse on the Dacres which promised the rapid extinction of the family. This was fulfilled when Thomas' young son fell from his vaulting-horse and was killed, and Thomas himself dyed soon afterwards. On his death the ghost of the maiden whom he had wronged ceased to walk in the meadows by the stream where she drowned. His widow became the third wife of the fourth Duke of Norfolk. Exactly the same story is told of another Dacre stronghold – Naworth Castle.

Yet another Dacre castle stands a short distance away, to the north of the A66: this is Greystoke where there are supposed to be two ghosts. One is a monk who is said to have been bricked up in a secret passage which led from the church to one of the bedrooms (unlikely, surely, for there to have been a groundfloor bedroom in a castle?). Anyway he

Aira Force

appears in the disused room occasionally, especially favouring the month of February.

When the Dacres lost their fortune, Greystoke became a property of the Howards, Dukes of Norfolk. Charles Howard, a Duke who was so keen on hunting that he broke the sabbath in the pursuit of game, once persuaded a house-guest to join him in sport on a Sunday. They had an excellent day, and after an evening of great hospitality the guest was shown to his bedroom – the same one, apparently, as that haunted by the unfortunate monk. He was never seen in earthly form again, but returns, so it is said, as a ghost on the anniversary of his disappearance.

Aira Force is one of the best-known beauty-spots of the Lakes, its legends probably contributing to its popularity. Wordsworth wrote a highly romantic poem called *The Somnambulist* about the waterfall, which concludes with the heroine, who had waited for many years for her betrothed to return to her after proving his valour and love in battle, being discovered sleepwalking beside the torrent by her lover. Not knowing whether she is real or a ghost he plucks at her shoulder:

> *The soft touch snapped the thread*
> *Of slumber – shrieking back she fell,*
> *And the Stream whirled her down the dell*
> *Along its foaming bed.*

Her lover eventually pulls her out of the stream and she expires in his arms, knowing that his love for her was true after all. He then builds himself a hermit's cell nearby and spends the rest of his days there 'From vain temptations free'.

De Quincey's story of an apparition at the Force is hardly less romantic, though at least it is more amusing. In *Recollections of the Lake Poets* he tells how a Miss Smith, who lived nearby, decided to explore the Force alone, and not with the usual guide. She felt herself to be a good 'cragswoman' and succeeded in climbing up beside the cataract for about half an hour. Then she found herself enclosed in 'an aerial dungeon' and, only managing to escape from this with difficulty, came to the brink of a chasm:

Retreat seemed in every direction alike even more impossible. Down the chasm, at least, she might have leaped, though with little or no chance of escaping with life; but on all other quarters it seemed to her eye that at no price could she effect an exit, since the rocks stood round her in a semi-circus, all lofty, all perpendicular, all glazed with trickling water, or smooth as polished porphyry.... Suddenly, however, as she swept the whole circuit of her station with her alarmed eye, she saw clearly, about two hundred yards beyond her own position, a lady in a white muslin morning robe, such as were then universally worn by young ladies until dinner-time. The lady beckoned with a gesture and in manner that, in a moment, gave her confidence to advance − *how* she could not guess; but, in some way that baffled all power to retrace it, she found instantaneously the outlet which previously had escaped her. She continued to advance towards the lady, whom now, in the same moment, she found to be standing on the other side of the *force*, and, also to be her own sister....

This apparition leads Miss Smith safely down to the path whereupon she vanished, leaving her to make the remainder of the descent alone. And when the 'adventurous cragswoman' reached home she found her sister 'in the same situation and employment in which she had left her; and the whole family assured her that she had never stirred from the house.'

From the head of Ullswater the main road climbs the Kirkstone Pass to take us to Ambleside and back to Chapter Four. The Pass itself afforded no shelter to travellers until the 1840s when the inn was built. This followed many tragic deaths in bad weather. Particularly sad was that of Ruth Ray who struggled up the Pass, carrying her child, having visited her sick father in Patterdale. When she failed to return home her husband set out into the blizzard to find her, and, stumbling through deep drifts of snow, would have perished too had he not been able to follow a sheepdog which led him to its master. In first light the shepherd and husband set about searching for the woman and child. The mother they found dead, but miraculously the babe survived: the brave mother had wrapped him snuggly into her cloak and shawl.

Finally, at the foot of the Pass just into Ambleside, there is a large house that was once a hotel (it is now a Charlotte Mason College). When it was a hotel, very many years ago, there was a fire in the topmost bedrooms and some of the staff were killed. The hotel was forced to close because the terrible smell of burning flesh would sometimes, and for no apparent reason, pervade the building.

Chapter Eight

# Carlisle and the North

The villages of Salkeld, Great and Little, lie to the east of the M6, about five miles to the north-east of Penrith. Long Meg and her Daughters, that 'family forlorn' as Wordsworth saw them, stand to the north of Little Salkeld, mysterious monuments of a civilisation which flourished here at least three and a half thousand years ago. Long Meg is the tallest of the stones, about three metres in height. She seems to have been given this name after a famous virago who lived in Westminster during the reign of King Henry VIII. At first the stones were believed to be Roman, then they were accredited to shadowy Druids, but now they are known to belong to the Bronze Age, though

Long Meg

the significance of the arrangement can only be guessed at. Many traditions cling to this remarkable stone circle:

If by any means a piece were broken off Meg, the unfortunate lady would bleed, and if any person could number the stones correctly, or twice reckon them the same, he would disenchant the Dulcinea of the moor and her daughters, or her lovers, as it might prove to be. But, strange to say, though many persons have come expressly to amuse themselves with the hope of bringing relief to Meg and her family, no one has yet succeeded. Somebody, it is said, once made a purchase of cakes with the intention of laying one on each stone, but whether his patience or his cakes failed him, we are not informed.

The late Colonel Lacy, it is said, conceived the idea of removing Long Meg and her Daughters by blasting. Whilst the work was being done with under his orders, the slumbering powers of Druidism rose in arms against this violation of their sanctuary, and such a storm of thunder and lightning, and such heavy rain and hail ensued, as the Fell-sides never before witnessed. The labourers fled for their lives vowing never more to meddle with Long Meg.

Two of the famous 'Lucks' of Lakeland belong to houses situated close to Salkeld − Edenhall and Burrell Green (*see* Chapter Six).

Renwick is a lonely village on the edge of the moors which culminate in the appropriately-named Fiends' Fell. It must have seemed like the last place on earth in the eighteenth century when the village saw few visitors. It was at this time that the church was rebuilt. Legend has it that as the higher fabric was being dismantled a horrifying creature flew out, a giant bat which the workmen took to be a cockatrice (an inferior form of dragon). They immediately downed tools and fled, but there was one of their number who was more practical and courageous. He cut down a bough from a nearby rowan tree and with this managed to defeat the unnatural beast. This hero, and his successors, were granted exemption from tithes for their property at Scale Houses, a reward for the slaying of the 'crackachrist', as it was described on the deeds. Local people, however, say that the creature is still to be seen or felt on dark nights, and there are some who fear it to be a vampire.

The classic British vampire story belongs to a neighbouring village, Croglin, and though well-known in the early part of this century has since been comparatively neglected. In his *Haunted Britain*, a

The new church at Renwick

gazetteer of ghosts, Antony Hippisley Coxe dismisses it as 'an unidentified solid apparition, said to be a vampire', and gets its address wrong, yet the story is an old one, certainly pre-dating Bram Stoker's *Dracula*, possibly by two hundred years or more. The earliest account of the story was printed in *The Story of my Life* by the Victorian gossip Augustus Hare. The first volume of this was published in 1896, a year before the appearance of *Dracula*. Several writers repeated Hare's account, notably Charles Harper in his famous work of the 1920s, *Haunted Houses*. He was the first to point out serious inconsistencies in Hare's story, and from then on the Croglin vampire fell into disrepute and neglect.

*Tomorrow* was an excellent journal of the paranormal that flourished in the 1950s and 60s. Its editor, F. Clive Ross, visited friends in Broughton-in-Furness in November 1962, and out of curiosity went to see Croglin. He discovered that the various discrepancies that had led earlier writers to dismiss the story of the vampire were invalid, and wrote a painstaking account that re-establishes the authenticity of the

Croglin Low Hall

original story. I am grateful to Mr Stephen White of the Carlisle Library for directing me to the article (*Tomorrow*, Vol. XI, No. 11).

The house concerned was called Croglin Grange by Augustus Hare, though this was a misnomer or a disguise and there can be little doubt that its real identity is Croglin Low Hall. According to Hare, the house had belonged to a family called Fisher for many generations. In time the Fishers outgrew their northern home, 'both in family and fortune', and went away to the south to live near Guildford, letting Croglin to two brothers and a sister.

They proved to be excellent tenants and became well-liked in the neighbourhood. The small size of the house, and its unusual plan (it was of only one storey) suited them, as did its secluded location tucked away in a fold of the hills some distance from the village. The first winter of their tenancy passed uneventfully, and nothing untoward occurred until midway through the following summer. The day in question had been hot and airless. After dinner the two brothers and their sister sat outside watching the sun set and the moon rise over the trees which separated the gardens from the churchyard. The story, as told to Augustus Hare by a member of the Fisher family, continues:

When they separated for the night, all retiring to their rooms on the ground floor (for, as I said, there was no upstairs in that house), the sister felt that the heat was so great that she could not sleep, and having fastened her window, she did not close the shutters – in that very quiet place it was not necessary – and, propped against the pillows, she still watched the wonderful, the marvellous beauty of the summer night. Gradually she became aware of two lights, two lights which flickered in and out of the belt of trees which separated the lawn from the churchyard, and, as her gaze became fixed upon them, she saw them emerge, fixed in a dark substance, a definite ghastly *something*, which seemed every moment to become nearer, increasing in size and substance as it approached. Every now and then it was lost for a moment in the long shadows which stretched across the lawn from the trees, and then it emerged larger than ever, and still coming on. As she watched it, the most uncontrollable horror seized her. She longed to get away, but the door was close to the window, and the door was locked on the inside, and while she was unlocking it she must be for an instant nearer to *it*. She longed to scream, but her voice seemed paralysed, her tongue glued to the roof of her mouth.

Suddenly – she could never explain why afterwards – the terrible object seemed to turn to one side, seemed to be going round the house, not to be coming to her at all, and immediately she jumped out of bed and rushed to the door, but as she was unlocking it she heard scratch, scratch, scratch upon the window. She felt a sort of mental comfort in the knowledge that the window was securely fastened on the inside. Suddenly the scratching sound ceased, and a kind of pecking sound took its place. Then, in her agony, she became aware that the creature was unpicking the lead! The noise continued, and a diamond pane of glass fell into the room. Then a long bony finger of the creature came in and turned the handle of the window, and the window opened, and the creature came in; and it came across the room, and her terror was so great that she could not scream, and it came up to the bed, and it twisted its long, bony fingers into her hair, and it dragged her head over the side of the bed, and – it bit her violently in the throat.

As it bit her, her voice was released, and she screamed with all her might and main. Her brothers rushed out of their rooms, but the door was locked on the inside. A moment was lost while they got a poker and broke it open. Then the creature had already escaped through the window, and the sister, bleeding violently from a wound in the throat, was lying unconscious over the side of the bed. One brother pursued the creature, which fled before him through the moonlight with gigantic strides, and eventually seemed to disappear over the wall into the churchyard. Then he rejoined his brother by the sister's bedside. She was dreadfully hurt, and her wound was a very definite one, but she was of strong disposition, not even given to romance or superstition, and when she came to herself she said, 'What has happened is most extraordinary and I am very much hurt. It seems inexplicable, but of course there *is* an explanation, and we must wait for it. It will turn out that a lunatic has escaped from some asylum and found his way here.' The wound healed, and she appeared to get well, but the doctor who was sent for to her would not believe that she could bear so terrible a shock so easily, and insisted that she must have a change, mental and physical; so her brothers took her to Switzerland.

Being a sensible girl, when she went abroad she threw herself at once into the interests of the country she was in. She dried plants, she made sketches, she went up mountains, and, as autumn came on, she was the person who urged that they should return to Croglin Grange. 'We have taken it', she said, 'for seven years, and we have only been there once; and we shall always find it difficult to let a house which is only one storey high, so we had better return there; lunatics do not escape every day.' As she urged it, her brothers wished nothing better, and the family returned to Cumberland. From there being no upstairs in the house it was impossible to make any great change in their arrangements. The sister occupied the same room, but it is unnecessary to say she always closed the shutters, which, however, as in many old houses, always left one top pane of the window uncovered. The brothers moved, and occupied a room together, exactly opposite that of their sister, and they always kept loaded pistols in their room.

The winter passed most peacefully and happily. In the following March, the sister was suddenly awakened by a sound she remembered only too well – scratch, scratch, scratch, upon the window, and, looking up, she saw, climbed up to the topmost pane of the window, the same hideous brown shrivelled face, with glaring eyes, looking in at her. This time she screamed as loud as she could. Her brothers rushed out of their room with pistols, and out of the front door. The creature was already scudding away across the lawn. One of the brothers fired and hit it in the leg, but still with the other leg it continued to make away, scrambled over the wall into the churchyard, and seemed to disappear into a vault which belonged to a family long extinct.

The next day the brothers summoned all the tenants of Croglin Grange, and in their presence the vault was opened. A horrible scene revealed itself. The vault was full of coffins; they had been broken open, and their contents, horribly mangled and distorted, were scattered over the floor. One coffin alone remained intact. Of that the lid had been lifted, but still lay loose upon the coffin. They raised it, and there, brown, withered, shrivelled, mummified, but quite entire, was the same hideous figure which had looked in at the windows of Croglin Grange, with the marks of a recent pistol-shot in the leg: and they did the only thing that can lay a vampire – they burnt it.

Harper, and other re-tellers of the tale who came after him, objected that the tale could not possibly be true for two reasons. Firstly, both Croglin Low Hall and Croglin High Hall are two-storey buildings. Secondly, in each instance the church lies a great distance (at least a mile-and-a-half as the crow flies) away from these houses.

Mr Clive Ross was aware of these discrepancies. The first place that he visited in Croglin was the unpretentious church, rebuilt in 1878. In its porch he found a typewritten sheet which gave a brief history of the village and the church. It concluded: 'Croglin Low Hall is the ancient Manor House of Old Croglin. It belonged to the Dacre family until 1589. There was a second church in Croglin here, probably serving as a private chapel to the house. Nothing of this church now exists.'

This quickly disposed of one of the objections. The other was less easily solved, though at Low Hall Mr Ross found some evidence to suggest that the building had once been of only one storey: large stone corbels jutting from the wall looked as though they had been intended to support a roof. By contacting the widow of the former owner of Low Hall, Mrs Parkin, he discovered further details to support the story.

The church close by Low Hall had been left ruined by Ireton, Cromwell's brother-in-law. It will be remembered that the Howards, who took over most of the Dacre estates, were a Catholic family. Mrs Parkin believed that the vampire story dated from between 1680 and 1690 when the church was in ruins but there were still graves and family vaults in the former churchyard. She said that at the time of the vampire's appearance the tenants of Croglin High Hall had a three-year-old daughter. She had been a fine healthy child but suddenly turned listless and pale, and her parents noticed what they took to be the bite-marks of a rat on her throat. After the attack on Miss Cranswell (for that was her name) at Low Hall, the child's father was one of the party who broke open the vampire's tomb. Mrs Parkin had also been told by a member of the Fisher family that the Hall had been a single-storey building until 1720 and was known as the Grange until this time.

A further unsolved mystery belonged to the house that might have some bearing on the tale of the vampire. When Mrs Parkin's husband had been alive a chimney had caught fire and threatened to set light to the rest of the building. Eventually the blaze was doused by the efforts of the two fire brigades who dashed to the scene, but to make sure that the fire was completely dead a stone was removed from the dining-room fireplace. In doing this a skeleton was discovered. Mr Parkin thought that this should be removed and re-interred in a Roman Catholic churchyard, but he died before this could be done. Consequently it seems that the skeleton is still there unless subsequent occupants of the Hall have had it removed.

To the north of Croglin is Cumrew, long famous for its ghosts and witches. Many of these were supposed to frequent Dunwalloght Castle, yet another Dacre stronghold, which was situated nearby.

The 'Radiant Boy' of Corby Castle is one of the most famous of the

Corby Castle

ghosts of Cumbria. No one knows who he is or why he appears, but only a few would welcome seeing him, for those who do usually achieve power and fortune but meet a violent end. The best-known victim of the visitation was Lord Castlereagh who became Foreign Minister before going insane and committing suicide in 1822. The 'Radiant Boy' is a beautiful child dressed in dazzling white who appears with an aura of unearthly light surrounding him. Corby was originally a pele tower built in the thirteenth century by the Salkeld family who sold out to the Howards in 1611. The present mansion dates from 1809.

In the previous chapter there is a reference to the A6, for long the major trunk road of the district, being haunted by a black dog at Shap. Before the construction of the motorway it was believed that the stretch of the A6 at Plumpton was also haunted, that unnatural lights would suddenly blaze from nowhere to blind drivers and so cause accidents. It was here, many years ago, that a villain named Toplis was eventually cornered by police and shot dead. He had murdered a London taxi driver.

Yet further northwards up the A6, just to the east of the main road, is the village of Cotehill. This was the home of John Whitfield, a highwayman who grew careless through success. In 1768 he shot a man in broad daylight but failed to see that a boy watched the incident who could recognise him. Thus he was brought to justice, and for his many crimes was gibbeted alive by the road on the fellside at Barrock. He swung in great agony in his cage for some days until the driver of a stage-coach shot him to end his misery, but ghostly screams have been heard since in the vicinity where he suffered his cruel punishment.

On the western side of the motorway, near Dalston, Hawksdale Hall is said to be haunted by the ghost of a boy who hung himself there. Two rooms were found to be shut up when the house was renovated many years ago. The restless spirit walks with a lantern on All Hallows Eve, coming out of the front door and disappearing into the River Caldew.

Everyone knows that John Peel, the most famous huntsman ever, lived at Caldbeck, on the northern boundary of the National Park. In his days the village had about three times the number of inhabitants it has today, most being employed in the woollen mills. It also had thirteen pubs (there is only the one today). In such places the Women's Institute thrives and does sterling service for local history. They unearthed, as it were, two ghosts: in Bushay House an

Caldbeck

unaccountable light was regularly seen in the garden, while in the Rectory the rattling of chains was often heard in one of the rooms facing the churchyard.

However Caldbeck's most famous ghost is its black dog, which particularly favours the lanes towards Branthwaite. It always appears close to a holly tree, dashing madly up the road until it vanishes, again by a holly. There is a second story concerning a black dog which appears as a portent to a local family. Should a member of the family see this ghostly hound he is sure to die the following day. It has been suggested that the two black dogs are one and the same creature.

Although Cumbria has its fair share of market towns, each serving its own hinterland, there is no arguing that Carlisle is the hub of the region. The Romans instantly recognised this bridging-point over the Eden as being vital strategically, and built their great defensive wall just to the north, adopting Carlisle as their administrative centre. Its position so close to an ever-restless border gave it a unique character: it was always a military base as well as a commercial city. Reflecting its ancient defensive anxieties, a labyrinth of secret tunnels ran beneath

Carlisle

streets and buildings. Because of the violence of its past there are good causes for ghosts here.

Yet the evidence for them is hardly overwhelming. All the oldest buildings – the castle, cathedral, and friary – are said to be haunted, yet there are few, if any, detailed accounts of these ghosts. A tunnel once connected the cathedral with the Friar's Tavern in Devonshire Street and this pub was haunted, while another with a ghost was the old Citadel Bar. But the ghost here only ever appeared once, ordered himself a beer and vanished by walking through a brick wall. The incident was reported by the *Evening News & Star* on 13 December 1976, where the ghost was described as being in eighteenth-century dress. It does not comment on how he took to twentieth-century beer, though walking through the wall may have been comment enough.

The best Carlisle ghost story is told by Gerald Findler in *Lakeland Ghosts*. Twenty-five years ago a man gave a lift to an old gentleman who was thumbing cars at Shap (the motorway had not then been built). In conversation they discovered a mutual interest in chess. The old man promised the car driver he would let him have a particularly interesting problem that he had been working on if he would call at his home, and he gave him an address. Should he be out he would leave the problem on a small piece of paper in a tobacco jar on the mantelpiece.

Later the same day the driver searched out the address. A lady answered his knock at the door and was startled when he explained why he had called. It turned out that the old gentleman had, in fact, died three days previously. Somewhat bemused by this, the car driver asked whether there was a tobacco jar on the mantelpiece. When she replied that there was, he told her to look inside it, and there she discovered the scrap of paper with the chess problem just as had been promised.

The west walls of the city are supposed to still harbour a ghost, a cavalier dressed immaculately in white who smiles at all who see him. Because of this local residents are quite fond of him. He is usually seen early in the morning, and vanishes as he approaches the wall itself. The perpetrators of one of Cumberland's most famous crimes met their ends at the old Carlisle Gaol in 1886. After a long chase across the county, which had moments of high farce even though it ended in tragedy with the death of a policeman, the villains were eventually cornered and brought to trial.

Rudge, Baker and Martin became known as the 'Netherby murderers' although their only connection with that place was the burglary that they had carried out in the great house there. Netherby Hall, situated on the south bank of the Esk, was a Graham house immortalised by Scott as the scene of Young Lochinvar's romantic adventures. The house was full of distinguished guests invited for the Longtown coursing week, and the gang, knowing that there would be much jewellery on display, had come up from the south intending to help themselves to as much as possible. In the event they were disturbed and put to flight, only having a comparatively meagre haul of some £250-worth (all of which was abandoned during the course of their flight). It was always maintained that the leader of the gang escaped capture, and certainly there were four men involved with the police in the first encounter. This took place on the northern outskirts of Carlisle, at Kingstown, where on the night of the raid two constables attempted to stop four men. Shots were fired at the policemen, and one was left badly wounded.

Four men evaded the police at the next checkpoint, just half a mile to the south at Moorville. After this the men took to walking along the railway track, thinking that this was unlikely to be so well guarded. However one brave policeman, Constable Fortune, was foolish enough to attempt to waylay the desperados. He was battered to the ground and left lying across the tracks. But it seems there must be good in even the most hardened villain, and within minutes one of them returned and moved his unconscious body off the rails, though by tipping him down the embankment such severe injuries were caused that he had to be invalided from the force.

The gang remained hidden during the next day, but in the evening they appeared at the little station at Calthwaite asking for trains to the south. When they were told that there were no trains that night, they made off down the main road towards Plumpton. They must have forgotten that railway stations were connected by the new electric telegraph, and the police constable from the next village, Plumpton, was alerted and set off to meet them. A shot was heard soon afterwards at the vicarage, and the policeman was found, fatally wounded, lying close to the road. The three (or was it four?) burglars continued their flight by taking to the railway tracks again. Rudge and Martin were eventually caught at Tebay when a slow-moving goods-train was stopped and searched. Baker managed to reach Lancaster before he was captured.

All three men suffered death by hanging at Carlisle Gaol in 1886, but only rested for a short time in their graves there. A new prison was built and the bodies had to be exhumed and reburied. This took place at 3.30 one morning, the horses drawing the macabre cortège wearing leather muffles on their hooves. Now this incident would hardly qualify for inclusion in a book of ghost stories except for a remarkable sequel. As has been mentioned earlier, the robbers' loot was abandoned early in their flight; neither would the condemned men tell of where it had been hidden. *The Cumberland Evening News* on 23 December 1965 told the story of the recovery of the jewellery. Lady Mabel Howard of Greystoke Castle was quite well known for her gift of second sight (an account in the *Proceedings of the Society for Psychical Research* in 1893 listed a number of her successful prophecies). Some time after the robbery Lady Mabel and her husband gave a house party at Greystoke, in the course of which it was suggested that Lady Mabel should attempt to discover, by using automatic writing, where the cache was hidden. Her pencil wrote: 'In the river under the bridge at Tebay'. This seemed unlikely at the time, but a search was made and the jewels were discovered. Unfortunately

HIS ROYAL HIGHNESS
*William Duke of Cumberland.*

'Butcher' Cumberland

Naworth Castle

it is not known who transmitted this message to Lady Mabel or when the seance took place. If it were after the executions it might have been sent by one of the burglars in a belated fit of remorse.

In the previous century Carlisle had witnessed a host of executions. After Bonnie Prince Charlie's disastrous expedition into England in 1745 he retreated northwards leaving a small garrison of four hundred in Carlisle to delay pursuit. They were unable to hold out against the forces of the Duke of Cumberland ('Butcher Cumberland') and were held prisoner here until the uprising came to its calamitous end at Culloden. Many more captives were then brought south to join them, being held in the cathedral as well as the castle in squalid conditions. Some died in captivity, some were transported, and many were executed at Harraby, now a south-eastern suburb of the city. Their deaths were as painful as they were demeaning. The sentence read:

> You and every one of the prisoners at the bar, return to the prison from whence you came, and from thence you must be drawn to the place of execution. When you come there you must be hanged by the neck, but not

until you are dead, for you must be cut down alive; then your bowels must be taken out and burned before your faces; your hands must be severed from your bodies and your bodies each be divided into four quarters, and these must be at the King's disposal; and God have mercy on your souls.

It is on record that only a small number of the victims were insensible after hanging, and some were even able to struggle with their executioners. A few survived to the final part of the sentence which must have made the executioner, William Stout of Hexham, especially proud of his skill. Just outside Brampton there is a monument marking the site of the Capon Tree where judges, on their way from Newcastle to Carlisle, would pause in their journey to feast from plump capons. More rebels were put to death here, amongst them General Howard, Governor of Carlisle Castle. An ancient pamphlet tells of the spirits of the rebels flitting about with airy ropes about their necks on each anniversary of the day of execution'. Perhaps a similar commemoration takes place amongst the bungalows and semis of Harraby.

Both Naworth Castle, close to Brampton, and that at Askerton, further to the north-east, were once Dacre fortresses: each have ghosts. The story of Naworth is identical to the one told of Dacre Castle itself (*see* previous chapter) though there is also the story of a witch's curse that has partly been fulfilled: 'When a bull shall toll the Lanercost Bell, and a hare bring forth on Naworth's hearth-stone, Lanercost shall fall, Naworth be burned down, and Dalstone Church be washed away.'

At least one of the unlikely events must have taken place, for Lanercost Priory fell into ruin after the Dissolution though the west end of its church is still used. This contains the tomb of Thomas, Lord Dacre, who commanded the horse at Flodden and died in 1526. The tomb was robbed of both coffin and corpse in 1775. At this time many of the vaults were lying open to the elements including that of 'a venerable gentleman with a long white beard'. Naworth suffered from a fire in 1844 though it was restored to its former glory by Salvin. Dalston Church still stands intact.

Askerton Castle, which passed from the Dacres to the Howards in the seventeenth century, had a White Lady who haunted the Park. She was that rare creature, a ghost that spoke. She once appeared in front of a horseman and grabbed his bridle. She told him that she would never let it go unless he gave a promise that should never be divulged, upon pain of death. Naturally the promise was forthcoming and the White Lady disappeared.

129

Chapter Nine

# Western Lakeland

Scafell Pike is the highest mountain in England, and because of this it is also probably the most frequented (witness the litter). The paths to its summit are well-worn and pass through a desert of rock devoid of vegetation. The mountain itself is hidden by lesser heights for much of the ascent, and many less exalted peaks provide better viewpoints, yet despite these disadvantages Scafell Pike remains a favourite excursion for most visitors, young and old alike, and certainly it takes them through terrain that is daunting in its savagery.

Rock-climbers take all this in their stride. They do not make for the tops but for the sheer faces, which call on all their reserves of courage

Scafell Pike

and strength. To reach these they often have to make a trek that would exhaust the humble fellwalker. Scafell Crag lies below the summit of Scafell, the neighbouring summit to the Pike and only a little lower. The Crag is a vertical cliff of clean rock about 500 feet high, which from the bottom looks utterly unassailable. However the fellwalker will find a hidden route that does not need ropes and pitons, by way of Lord's Rake and the West Wall.

But it was a rock-climber that experienced a strange premonition here during the First World War. The story comes from *In Mountain Lakeland* by A.H. Griffin:

His closest friend had been one of the outstanding rock-climbers of his age and had gone away to fight for his country in France. One day the man who told the story had been climbing on Scafell Crag and on the way down Hollow Stones in the sunshine of a lovely summer afternoon he was unexpectedly joined by his old friend – unexpected because he had not heard that he was at home on leave. They walked down the fells side by side talking of the days they would have together when the war was over, and then the soldier had to cross over into another valley, promising he would see the other later. For days the man thought about his old friend and then one day he had a letter from France. The friend had been killed in action (or had died on active service) – on the very afternoon that the man who told the story positively believed he had talked with him on the way down to Wasdale Head. You and I may be unable to offer any explanation, but the storyteller believed that his great friend had been granted, at the very moment of death, a last sight of the hills he loved and a last chat with his closest friend.

A famous story is told of macabre happenings on the Corpse Road along which the folk of Wasdale Head used to take their dead for burial in Eskdale. Throughout Lakeland there were particular routes that had to be used by funeral processions: custom often dictated a route not normally used and this sometimes even meant the dismantling of fences. It was thought that any deviation from the traditional path would be a bad omen. Bodies were either carried on sleds or were strapped to the backs of pack-horses. On the famous occasion at Wasdale Head the horse carrying the body of a young man bolted somewhere on the remote and windswept Burnmoor and vanished into a swirling mountain mist. The bearers eventually had to return to the cottage of the dead man's mother and tell of their mishap.

Wasdale Head

The shock of this was too much for her to bear and she died shortly afterwards. Again a coffin was strapped to the back of a horse and the funeral party set out for Eskdale. On Burnmoor they encountered a terrible snowstorm, and in the midst of this the horse bolted with the poor woman's body. This was never recovered though the horse bearing her son's coffin was found by a search-party. It is said that a ghostly horse bearing a coffin on its back may be seen on stormy nights on Burnmoor, but few would be foolish enough to venture out to this remote spot in times of bad weather.

A favourite Lake District legend is that mentioned earlier in connection with Bewley Castle, where a would-be robber is killed by having hot tallow poured down his throat while he is asleep. A variation on this was told of a farm called Bakerstead in Miterdale. The spot where the farm stood is haunted by a fearsome boggle who roams abroad in perpetual death agonies. He never speaks a word, but 'snores and makes frightful choking sounds.' He not only sounds bad, but looks even worse, for so much tallow was poured over his face that his head is a huge and shapeless white blob. This is the ghost of the

Climbers' graves, Wasdale Head

thief who intended to rob the farm but was forestalled by the farmer's wife and her pot of boiling wax.

Styhead Pass carries the path that leads from Borrowdale to Wasdale Head – a dramatic way with the crags of Scafell Pike and Great Gable towering above. This is supposed to be haunted by the ghost of a long-dead outlaw named Bjorn, who was executed nearby. The original name of Sprinkling Tarn was 'the tarn of the branded Bjorn' and seems to illustrate the remarkable extent of Viking influence into these high mountain fastnesses.

Muncaster Castle, away from the mountains and on the coast at Ravenglass, has one of the famous Lucks of Cumbria mentioned earlier. Ruskin called Muncaster 'the gateway to Paradise' and it was a favourite place with the Prince of Wales, later King Edward VII, who frequently visited the Pennington-Ramsdens. The Castle was rebuilt by Anthony Salvin in the mid-nineteenth century, the ancient pele tower being incorporated into the enlarged structure, which unlike some of Salvin's other work, is never overbearing or pompous.

The castle is said to be haunted by the ghost of Thomas Skelton, the 'late Fool of Muncaster', who died c.1600. The splendid portrait of

'Thomas Skelton, late fool of Muncaster'

Skelton, holding his Last Will and Testament, may be seen by visitors to the Castle. It was his behaviour as jester that gave us the word 'tomfoolery', though he was allegedly a vicious and evil man. One story says that his master, Sir Ferdinand Pennington, paid him to kill a poor young carpenter who was making advances to his daughter. Skelton disposed of the unwelcome suitor with the utmost brutality, presenting the head to Sir Ferdinand as proof. Ever since, a ghost without a head has haunted the Tapestry Room in the castle, eternally seeking a lost love.

Earlier, in 1463, it was Sir John Pennington who sheltered the fugitive King Henry VI after the Lancastrian defeat at Hexham. Fleeing westwards across the freezing wastes of Lakeland the King had first begged sanctuary from the Irtons who lived in a hall on Irt Side to the west of Wastwater. The lady who refused the 'holy Monarch', the wife of John Irton, used to haunt a room at the Hall, dressed in black.

Egremont has a ghost of a pony and rider that only appears on Christmas Eve and whose origins may go back to the Middle Ages. The ghostly rider is said to be a fellfarmer who took rather too much Christmas ale in an Egremont tavern before hauling himself onto his horse and making his way back to his remote hill farm. Neither man nor beast were ever seen again in earthly form.

In *Lakeland Ghosts*, Gerald Findler writes of strange goings-on at a tannery in Egremont about forty years ago. Nine people swore that they saw a white mist rise from the ground which took on human shape and floated down the road until it came to the tannery, where a smaller misty figure joined it. Both then faded through the door of the building. As I am at the moment writing this in an old tannery, I feel able to vouch that *anything* can happen in such places.

Moresby is a small village just to the north of Whitehaven. The Hall at Moresby belonged to the Fletchers, one of whom supported the Jacobites in the 1715 Uprising. After the failure of the rebellion, he was abruptly taken to London to be questioned about his actions in the affair. However he was a secretive man and had neglected to tell his family that he was sheltering a fellow supporter of the cause in a secret room. This poor creature must have suffered a terrible death, by thirst and starvation, for the door of the room was locked from the outside and his erstwhile host had no means of sending a message to tell of his guest's predicament. The ghost of the locked-up Jacobite is said to still haunt one of the bedrooms of the Hall.

Workington Hall is a sad shell now. It became derelict after the last of the Curwens, Miss Isabel, got married in 1923. During the Second World War it served as an army billet, and afterwards, in advanced dilapidation, it was given to the Borough Council. In fairness, they spent a small fortune trying to stop the ravages of damp and woodworm (the intention was to use it as a Town Hall) but in 1968 work was abandoned and it was left to vandals to ruin the building beyond redemption.

The Hall was interesting architecturally as well as for its historic connections. Mary, Queen of Scots slept here on her last night of freedom before nineteen long years of captivity which ended with her execution at Fotheringhay. The token (The Luck of Workington) she gave the Curwens in gratitude for their hospitality may be seen at Belle Isle, Windermere. Yet it was not her poor spirit that might have been seen in this house, but that of her host, 'Galloping Harry'. (I am afraid I am unable to explain this nickname.) When the Curwens deserted the Old Faith (a Miss Curwen married Fairfax, the Cromwellian general, possibly to save the estate from confiscation), Sir

Belle Isle, Windermere

Harry's portrait was kept facing the wall. Perhaps this was the reason for his ghost to haunt the house, though an alternative explanation was put forward by John F. Curwen in 1899:

It seems that when Galloping Harry was nigh unto death, a French lady and her maid took him by his heels and pulled the old man down the stairs to a lower room, where they seated him in a high-backed chair.

Telling the servants that their master was much better and was not to be disturbed, they immediately decamped with all the available jewellery and embarked in a small vessel from the harbour.

Fifty years later, an old woman appeared in Workington and reported that she had been the maid, that their vessel had been wrecked off the Scilly Isles, her mistress drowned, the valuables lost and that she herself, having been saved by a French fishing smack, had taken the veil to find peace in a convent. She had now come back again to unburden her soul and die.

The ghostly disturbance at the Hall was the sound of Galloping Harry's head bumping down the stairs.

There were other signs of this being a well-disturbed house. This report appeared in a local paper thirty years ago:

When the last of the Curwens was in residence at the Hall, there had been a shooting party in the High Woods, and the privileged few who had taken part were enjoying a drink in the library. Amongst them was Patricius Lamplugh Curwen, Rector of Workington. On the rug before the great fire lay a couple of spaniels which had been doing their work during the day's shoot.

The conversation flagged a little, then suddenly the two dogs rose to their feet and stared at the door in the corner of the room. The door (if I remember correctly) was one which was almost a secret door because it was cut into one of the great library pictures, and it opened slowly.

The human occupants of the room saw nothing, but the dogs had their eyes on something which moved from the door to a vacant chair by the fireside, and then, for a while, they remained with their eyes fixed on that chair.

Then the dogs shifted their gaze as what they were seeing moved slowly back to the door which then closed, and things returned – as nearly as they could in the circumstances – to normal.

That was a sensation experienced by several visitors to the Hall, and there is no reason to doubt that there was 'something' in it. I was told the story by Canon Curwen himself, and he wasn't joking . . .

Between Workington and Cockermouth, the village of Brigham used to have a churchyard haunted by the ghost of Joseph Wilson, the Carlisle hangman, who drowned himself at Cockermouth in 1757. Once the headstone was decorated with a hangman's rope, but grisly-minded souvenir-hunters eroded this away over the years. The ghost of Wilson haunted the churchyard until about 1860 when the sexton became tired of the troublesome spirit and dug up the skull. He took it to the cottage where Wilson had lived and gave it to the occupants, two cloggers. They kept it in a wooden box in an antique cupboard, and, as far as is known, the ghost of the hangman never walked again.

Cass Howe is a small hill by the side of the road that leads southwards from Cockermouth towards Lorton. There is a story of a farmer from that village who was making his unsteady way home after a 'heavy' market day. As he approached Cass Howe he became aware that he was not alone: by his side was a man whose head lolled unnaturally upon his shoulders. When he realised that a noose was still attached to the man's neck, and that this must be a hanged man, the farmer took off down the lane as fast as his legs would carry him.

For all his efforts the man kept close to his elbow, begging him 'Stop, I want to speak to you.' He ran with long springy strides, easily keeping up with the terrified farmer, who eventually collapsed in a senseless heap at the side of the road, only to be discovered the next day.

The story of the boggle is this: once a Lorton man got so tired of his nagging wife that he decided to hang himself. But he was not even allowed to do this for himself, and she followed him down the lane, incessantly dwelling on all his shortcomings. At Cass Howe he climbed a tree, slung the rope over a branch, and began to put the noose around his neck. Telling him to 'Get on with it,' the wife turned and walked away. Still wishing to get just one kind word from her, the husband began to untie the rope, calling 'Stop, I want to talk to you,' but slipped with the knot still tied, and fell to his death.

Tallentire Hall is also close to Cockermouth: this was haunted by the headless ghost of a young girl who was murdered at the place. A correspondent to the old journal *Notes & Queries* explained the story and added that below the window of the room where the murder was supposed to have taken place, there was always a strange growth of a red fungus, known there as 'the Ghost's Blood'. This phenomenon may have been due to the bacteria *Serratia marcescens*, which has played a notable role in history. It may well have been this bug that turned up, like drops of blood, in the bread of the troops of Alexander the Great besieging Tyre in 332 BC. Inspired by this omen they were revitalised and took the city. In Christian times the appearance of a blood-like substance in the bread of the Eucharist has been taken as a sign of divine approval, a moment captured by Raphael in *The Mass at Bolsena*, where a doubting priest has his faith renewed when drops of blood are seen on the bread offered in celebration. In this century the same microbe has been extensively used as a marker in bacteriological experiments. Because of this it has grown increasingly resistant to antibiotics and has recently been the cause of serious infections in hospitals.

A house called Green Bank at Tallentire is also haunted. A girl of nineteen stayed there in 1951, sleeping on a camp bed in the little 'sitting room' on the ground floor. In the night her bed was shaken so violently by some unseen force that she had to abandon the room. Later she learned that there was a macabre story attached to the house. It had been used as a morgue after a disaster.

Wigton has the reputation of being the most haunted town in Cumbria. Its ghosts have intriguing names: the Church Street

Phantom, the Clinic Ghost, the Burnfoot Spirit, the Water Street Boggle, the New Street Headless Horror, and others.

The Kildare Court Boggle was an ominous ghost. When the Conservative Club (later the Kildare Hotel) was being built in the 1880s this boggle made an appearance. This is an eye-witness' account of what followed:

> The boggle had always been regarded as an omen of disaster, and so it proved to be in that instance.
>
> My father (a boy then) was one of a group of people watching hunks of dressed stone being pulled up by block, chain, and tackle to the top of the building.
>
> A Mr Johnston took the quickest way to the top by standing on a block being hoisted upwards. Unfortunately the chain broke at a height of between fifty and eighty feet. Although Mr Johnston landed on his feet, he died of internal injuries.

The Crown and Mitre was another hostelry with an unpleasant reputation. It had a sealed-up room known as 'the Suicide Room' which generated weird noises at night. Once the landlord's daughter tried to sleep in the neighbouring room. She woke up in the middle of the night, stretched out a hand for the candle, and touched instead a cold and clammy human face.

An old ivy-covered building near South End was the scene of a dreadful murder when a madman killed his wife and family with an axe. The place is haunted by the ghosts of the murderer's victims.

At Greenhill there was a ghost which delighted in extinguishing the lights on carriages and bicycles in the days before electric lighting, and the Dancing Boggle of Westnewton would seize late travellers and whirl them round 'in a merry reel'. Tom Jackson, an inveterate collector of ghost stories from these parts, told a story of phantom lights that he once encountered at Westnewton. Cycling home to Wigton he met with the eery light at Crossrigg and followed it all the way to Langrigg (the home of a different Headless Horror), the light keeping ten yards ahead all the way. The light vanished abruptly when he reached the top of the hill. He had another encounter with a phantom light at Longburn (should this be Longburgh?) where a hideous murder had taken place. The weapon used, a billhook, was exhibited in a shop window at Wigton.

Boltongate, a few miles to the south of Wigton, has a legend of

fairies mischievously turning the church around one night. A less pleasant story concerns a vicar falling out with the local squire, so seriously that the priest was eventually defrocked. There was no justice in this, and the sad result was that the vicar shot himself, but not before he had thoroughly cursed the squire, his family and descendants, and his house – Killnowe Manor. Each and every condition of the curse was fulfilled so that today nothing remains of what was once one of the loveliest mansions in the whole of 'the John Peel Country'.

Skinburness is a tiny village situated on the estuary known as Moricambe, which in fact serves two rivers on their passage to the sea, the poetically-named rivers Waver and Wampool (they sound like a partnership of eccentric solicitors). Once the place was of a much greater size, a thriving Solway port, but in 1302 a devastating storm swept Skinburness away, and the present village grew up some considerable distance from the site of the original, now submerged. There used to be a hazardous ferry-route across the Solway from Skinburness to a point between Annan and Gretna, one often used by runaway lovers fleeing to Gretna for a secret marriage. Once the boat was lost in these tide-tumbled waters and the screams of the drowning lovers may be heard above the wild sounds of wind and waves on stormy nights.

Another ghost story of the Solway concerns a slave ship named the *Betsy Jane* which was returning to her home-port of Whitehaven loaded with a rich cargo of ivory and gold, bought with the proceeds from the inhuman slave trade. She was wrecked just before reaching home, and local seafarers used to speak of seeing her last moments re-enacted, invariably at Christmas time.

Elliott O'Donnell also wrote of another doomed ship being seen in the Solway, the sailing-ship *Rotterdam*, which went down with all hands some time in the early years of the last century.

The Irruption of Solway Moss, which occurred in 1771, had a geological rather than supernatural cause, though at the time it must have seemed like the end of the world to those who witnessed it. The Moss is a peat-bog between the River Esk and the Scottish border, the scene of a terrible battle in 1542. Thomas Pennant described the strange event in his *Tour of Scotland & Voyage to the Hebrides* in 1772:

> Solway Moss consists of sixteen hundred acres; lies some height above the cultivated tract, and seems to have been nothing but a collection of thin

peaty mud: the surface itself was always so near the state of a quagmire, that in most places it was unsafe for any thing heavier than a sportsman to venture on, even in the driest summer.

The shell or crust that kept this liquid within bounds, nearest to the valley, was at first of sufficient strength to contain it: but by the imprudence of the peat-diggers, who were continually working on that side, at length became so weakened, as not longer to be able to resist the weight pressing on it. . . .

Late in the night of the 17th of November of the last year, a farmer, who lived nearest the Moss, was alarmed with an unusual noise. The crust had at once given way, and the black deluge was rolling towards his house, when he was gone out with a lantern to see the cause of his fright, he saw the stream approach him; and first thought that it was his dunghill, that by some supernatural cause, had been set in motion; but soon discovering the danger, he gave notice to his neighbours with all expedition: but others received no other advice but what this Stygian tide gave them: some by its noise, many by its entrance into their houses, and I have been assured that some were surprised with it even in their beds: these passed a horrible

night, remaining totally ignorant of their fate, and the cause of their calamity, till the morning, when their neighbours, with difficulty, got them out through the roof. About three hundred acres of moss were thus discharged, and above four hundred of land covered; the houses either overthrown or filled to their roofs; and the hedges overwhelmed; but providentially not a human life (was) lost; several cattle were suffocated; and those which were housed had very small chance of escaping. The case of a cow is so singular as to deserve mention. She was the only one out of eight, in the same cow-house, that was saved, after having stood sixty hours up to the neck in mud and water: when she was relieved, she did not refuse to eat, but would not taste water: nor could she even look at it without showing manifest signs of horror.

The irruption burst from the place of its discharge, like a cataract of thick ink; and continued in a stream of the same appearance, intermixed with great fragments of peat, with their heathy surface; then flowed like a tide charged with pieces of wreck, filling the whole valley, running up every little opening, and on its retreat, leaving upon the shore tremendous heaps of turf, memorials of the height this dark torrent arrived at. The farther it flowed, the more room it had to expand, lessening in depth, till it mixed its stream with that of the Esk.